MW01129560

Deceived

(THE WICKED WOODLEYS BOOK 2)

By

USA Today Bestseller
Jess Michaels

DECEIVED
The Wicked Woodleys Book 2

For more information, contact Jess Michaels
www.AuthorJessMichaels.com
PO Box 814, Cortaro, AZ 85652-0814

To contact the author:
Email: Jess@AuthorJessMichaels.com
Twitter www.twitter.com/JessMichaelsbks
Facebook: www.facebook.com/JessMichaelsBks

Jess Michaels raffles a FREE Kindle or Amazon gift certificate EVERY month to members of her newsletter, so sign up on her website:
http://www.authorjessmichaels.com/join-the-jess-michaels-newsletter/

DEDICATION

To the boy who saved me from all my own fears that I couldn't be loved. Michael, you are my hero.

PROLOGUE

1800

Lord Evan, second son of the late Marquis of Woodley, sat beside the lake on his family's country estate watching the prettiest girl he'd ever seen come strolling to the water's edge. She had come to his family estate for his mother's gathering. Right now on the veranda all the adults were holding court and speaking of boring things. His older brother by two years, Edward, was a part of that, forced into their company by the fact that he had inherited the title of marquis a year before.

But Evan? Evan was glad not to be there. He was much happier here.

"What's that girl's name?" Evan asked, elbowing his younger brother Gabriel.

"Who?" Gabriel asked, looking up from the muddy puddle he was poking with a stick. He shielded his gaze from the sun and shook his head. "That's Claire, stupid."

Evan gritted his teeth. Gabriel was only ten and rather obtuse when it came to girls. "Not her, of course. The girl with them."

"Josie?" Gabriel rolled his eyes. "She and Claire have been best friends forever—you'd think you'd know that."

"I *do* know it. I mean the older girl. Who is the *older* girl?" Evan asked again.

Gabriel seemed to search the massive collection of data

I

that made up his sharp mind and shrugged. "I think Mama said her name was...was...Aurora. She's Lord Aldridge's daughter. But she's two years older than you are, Evan. She'll never notice you."

Evan arched a brow. "Is that a challenge?"

"Everything is for you." Gabriel rolled his eyes and promptly returned to his mud puddle where he would likely stay.

Evan grinned. What his brother said was true. While Edward was serious and studious and Gabriel was already observing everything around them, Evan's claim to fame in the Woodley clan was that he never refused a bet or an opportunity to prove someone wrong about himself.

And now was the perfect time to do just that. Because Aurora, Claire and Josie had just reached the lake's edge.

"*Ladies*," Evan said with a flair he'd seen some dashing gentlemen use. Claire rolled her eyes and Aurora's flicked slightly to his, but Josie let out a wide smile.

"Hello Evan," she said, edging toward him.

Evan frowned. Josie and Claire were best friends and she was three years younger than him. It wasn't that he didn't like Josie—not at all. She was fine enough company, he supposed. But she liked him a bit too much, and while most days he just ignored it...perhaps even enjoyed it a little, today he didn't want Aurora getting the wrong idea.

"Josie," he grunted, and moved away from her toward Aurora.

Two more different girls there could not have been, really. While fifteen-year-old Aurora was willowy and fair, with golden ringlets that were arranged just so, Josie was short and plump, her brown locks somewhat flat and her nose sprinkled with freckles.

Though why he compared the two girls, he didn't know. After all, Josie was nothing but a nuisance.

"Lady Aurora," he said, pushing all his thoughts away and smiling at the girl who held his interest. "Aren't you lovely today?"

She shrugged. "I'm lovely every day."

He laughed at her quip for a moment before she glared at him. Oh. So she didn't mean the comment to be amusing. He frowned. So she was a little vain. Why wouldn't she be?

"I cannot imagine that isn't true," he said, scrambling to recover from the annoyance he had put in her eyes. "Are you enjoying our estate?"

"It really is the prettiest place," Josie interrupted, moving forward again. Her hands were clasped before her and her eyes rapt as she stared around the grounds.

Claire laughed a little. "It's hardly different from your father's home, Josie, which is only, what? Five miles away?"

Josie shook her head. "Oh, no. His estate is nothing compared to this! This place has always been a fairyland to me."

At that, Aurora snorted out a laugh. "Well, I suppose *some* of us still need baby fairy stories. If I had your life, Josie, I would believe in them too."

Evan jerked his gaze from Aurora's face to Josie's and saw his sister's friend crumple ever so slightly, but then she lifted her chin. "I never said I believed in fairy stories, Aurora. I only said that this place put me to mind of them sometimes."

Aurora folded her arms. "Well, what of you?" She tossed her chin in Evan's direction and he realized she was directing her question to him. Ah, just what he'd been waiting for!

"I'm certainly too old for fairytales," he said as he sidled closer to her. From the corner of his eye, he saw Josie's face fall further but ignored it. He couldn't be responsible for sensitive little Josie Westfall's moods. Right now he had to focus on matters at hand.

But Josie didn't seem to be deterred by the older girl's teasing. She moved closer too. "You needn't judge, Aurora. It wasn't so many years ago you used to dress up and dance around like fairies too!"

Aurora's face went from one of pretty and pleasing to an

3

DECEIVED

expression of anger so swiftly that it took Evan off guard. She spun on Josie and the younger girl recoiled slightly, stepping closer to Claire.

"*You* shut your mouth," Aurora growled.

Claire caught her friend's hand. "Leave her alone, Aurora."

"She should stay out of it, though," Evan offered, smiling at Aurora. "Aurora is too old for your baby games."

"They aren't baby games—" Josie began.

"Oh, stop, Horsey," Evan said, and then clapped a hand over his mouth. He hadn't meant to say "Horsey"—it had been a slip of the tongue.

"What did you call me?" Josie asked slowly, the color draining from her face.

Aurora began to laugh, her eyes welling up with mirth-filled tears. "Horsey! Oh God, it's perfect. Horsey Josie Westfall. How are you, Horsey? Can I get you something? A bucket of oats, perhaps?"

Claire jumped in front of her friend. "Stop that!"

Both Claire and Josie looked toward Evan and he saw the twin expressions of expectation on their faces. And now he was in a conundrum. He could correct Aurora, tell her not to bully Josie. But that would certainly end any chance he had to impress the older girl.

He slowly found himself shrugging. "Aw, come on, Josie. Don't be such a baby."

The next moment seemed to move in slow motion. Aurora laughed and laughed in the background, a wicked accompaniment to how Josie's face crumpled with humiliation and disappointment. Her green eyes filled with tears and she glared at Evan, pinning him in his spot, making him so very aware of how ungentlemanly he was being at present.

"Come on," Claire said, catching her friend's arm. "Let's go up to the house."

"Or the stables!" Aurora cackled. "Prance away, Horsey!"

Josie let out a pained sound as she stumbled back up the

hill toward the house with Claire. Evan watched them for a moment, tossed a glance back at Aurora, who suddenly seemed less pretty as she stood laughing hysterically at Josie. Then he bolted forward to catch up with his sister and her friend.

"Wait, Josie!" he called out.

They ignored him and kept walking, and he hustled faster to get in front of them.

"Josie," he said. "Don't be upset. We were just teasing."

"No, you weren't," Josie whispered, her eyes away from his.

He swallowed, guilt making him defensive. "You're overreacting!"

Now she looked at him. Well, glared at him. "I expected *her* to be mean, but not you."

"Yes, you were awful," Claire agreed.

He shoved his hands in his pockets and stared down at his shoes. "You won't even let me apologize?"

"You aren't sorry," Josie said softly, though her voice trembled. "And I will never forgive you. Ever."

And with that she shook off Claire's arm and began to run toward the house, Claire at her heels. Evan hesitated as they went, a strange urge to follow them burning inside of him.

But behind him there was a siren's call.

"Your name is Evan, isn't it?" came Aurora's voice.

He slowly faced her. She really wasn't as pretty as he had first thought, but there was a smirking smile on her face now. An inviting look that made him take a step toward her anyway.

"Yes," he said slowly.

"Well, are you going to take me on a turn around the lake?" she asked.

He looked back over his shoulder. Claire and Josie were gone from view. He should go after them. But the older girl was tempting.

So he held out an arm for Aurora and promptly pushed aside all his discomfort about how he had treated Josie. After all, he'd have plenty of chances to make it up to Josie. She liked him, she'd forgive him soon enough.

CHAPTER ONE

1816

Evan speared a perfectly cooked sausage link and cut into it with gusto. "Great God, Mrs. Ford is the best cook in the empire," he said. "I must have her come and give lessons at my London home."

His younger sister Audrey laughed. "I'm sure your cook would love that."

"Yes, there is nothing a person—a servant—loves more than to be told they need to learn their job," Audrey's fiancé and their longtime family friend Jude Samson said drily.

"Mrs. Ford does outdo herself," their oldest brother Edward said as he swirled a piece of toast through the yolk left on his plate. "But that is more for Mama than for us."

Evan smiled, but his jovial mood faded slightly. The reason they were all at the country estate, Briarlake Cross, was because of their mother. The dowager had fallen gravely ill just over a month before and they had nearly lost her. Even now she was still weak in her recovery.

"How do you think she is?" Evan asked.

At that moment, Edward's new wife Mary stepped into the room. Evan watched as she gave his brother a secret smile meant just for him before she addressed the room at large.

"I can answer that," Mary said, taking her spot beside her

husband and beaming as he stood and set about filling her a plate from the sideboard. "She is very well, I think. Just overly tired this morning. She's taking her tray upstairs with Miss Gray as company."

Juliet Gray was the healer who had saved their mother's life. The entire family owed the young woman a debt.

"Miss Gray is here?" Gabriel asked, sitting up slightly and joining the conversation for the first time that morning. Their brother had been melancholy for weeks.

And Evan couldn't blame him. Their sister Claire, Gabriel's twin, had been missing for nearly two years after an unfortunate marriage. Just a few weeks before, they had nearly found her, but she'd disappeared once more.

"She is," Mary said softly, and Evan saw her watching Gabriel closely. She was a new addition to their family, but already she had the same care and worry for them as anyone could hope for.

"Do you think that the wedding will be too much for her?" Audrey asked. "It is only a few days away."

At the question, everyone at the table began to smile. How could they not? Audrey's impending nuptials to Jude Samson, whom the entire family had long considered a brother, were cause for much joy, even if their "courtship" had not been usual.

"No," Edward said with an encouraging smile for Audrey as he handed over Mary's plate and retook his spot. "I spoke to her at length about it last night. She is very much looking forward to it. We will all be mindful of her condition and Miss Gray will attend to ensure she is not overly excited."

"The wedding itself is a small affair anyway," Jude reassured his future bride, taking her hand in his and smiling down at her. "Just family and the barest few friends. And if the gathering she has planned for afterward gets to be too much for her, I'm sure Miss Gray will insist on making her rest."

Audrey smiled up at him adoringly, but then shook her head as if clearing it. "Oh, that reminds me. I will have to tell the staff that they should make space for two more guests at the ceremony."

"Two more?" Edward asked. "Who else have you decided to include?"

"Josie and her mother," Audrey said. "I thought it would be nice to have them here."

Gabriel and Evan both tensed, though Evan thought their anxieties stemmed from very different sources. Likely Gabriel was reminded of Claire by the mention of Josie's name, since the two had been best friends.

But Evan was reminded of something very different.

He took a long sip of his coffee before he said, "Jocelyn Westfall, you mean?"

Audrey wrinkled her brow as she stared at him. "Do you know many other Josies?" she teased.

"I suppose I don't," he said, hoping his reaction wasn't totally clear on his face. After all, Josie was normally a source of frustration for him. He hadn't seen her in several years, even before Claire disappeared. And he hadn't exactly been sorry about that fact. "Why are you inviting her? It would be quite the trek for her and her mother."

Audrey shrugged. "When Mary and I were in the village yesterday, we saw Mrs. Westfall's butler, Mr. Charles. He was always such a friendly man and he said he had arrived ahead of them to prepare the country estate. They should be here from London this afternoon."

Evan gripped his leg beneath the table. "I see. And you're inviting her to your family wedding."

Audrey hesitated slightly and her gaze flitted down to her plate. "She was like family growing up. She and Claire were thick as thieves. Having her here would be a bit like—"

She cut herself off abruptly, but the entire table knew what she meant. Including Evan, who promptly began to hate himself for making Audrey say out loud a pain he wished she didn't feel. He cleared his throat before he forced a grin.

"Josie Westfall despises me, you know."

Audrey glanced up and her eyes were suddenly brighter. "I know," she said as she got to her feet. "But *you're* invited anyway." He threw a hand up to his chest with a dramatic gasp that set Audrey to laughing. "And now I must go up to Mama. I promised to show her the final stitching on the veil for the wedding."

Mary leapt up, plate of food half uneaten. "Oh, I will come too! I cannot wait to see the final product."

"But you've hardly—" Edward began, but Mary cut him off by leaning down to press a kiss to his forehead.

"I know, I know. I'll have a very hardy luncheon, I assure you," she laughed as she caught Audrey's hand and the two left the room. For a few moments, they could all hear the peals of giggles coming from the two women in the distance.

"That girl will drive me to distraction," Edward muttered, though he exchanged a knowing smile with Jude across the table.

"The very best kind of distraction," Jude responded with a smile just as telling.

Gabriel rolled his eyes as he reached across to Mary's abandoned plate and took an uneaten sausage link from it. "You two. I swear, you are like puppies."

"Oh, don't listen to Gabriel," Evan said with a half-smile for the other two men. "He's just being broody and dramatic."

"I don't brood," Gabriel said, though the glare he tossed Evan certainly didn't make his case.

Evan shrugged. "One of us should. Great God, it used to be Edward, but now he flits around all in love and happy. That leaves the brooding to you, brother."

"And why not you?" Gabriel asked, though the corners of his lips had begun to twitch as the conversation went on. It was good to see after the past few weeks—hell, *years*—of disappointment and sadness.

"I'd make a terrible brooder," Evan said with a shrug. "I don't have a dark bone in my body, I fear."

"Truly?" Jude asked, joining in the fun. And he could

since he had been part of their clan for what seemed like forever. Marrying Audrey would only solidify his place as the fourth Woodley brother.

"Why do you look so incredulous?" he demanded.

Edward was the one who responded. He laughed as he said, "'Josie Westfall despises me!'" Then he threw his hand up to his forehead and tossed his head back with great dramatic flair, setting off laughter from Jude and Gabriel.

Evan shifted in his chair. "Now wait a moment…"

"Oh, you cannot deny it. You were all dramatics when asking about her," Jude interrupted. "You should have seen your eyes."

Folding his arms, Evan stared straight ahead. "I don't know what you're talking about. You're being an idiot."

"Why *does* she hate you so much anyway?" Edward asked. "I've never understood it."

For a brief moment, Evan flashed back to a much-recalled and highly despised afternoon sixteen years ago. Flashed back to the bright pain in Josie's eyes. Then he blinked those thoughts away, along with the shame that accompanied them.

"I don't know," he lied. "Miss Westfall has the memory of an elephant, I suppose. Never forgets a slight."

"You slighted her?" Jude said with wide eyes.

"I don't know. She hates me, I must have," Evan said, waving away their questions. "Or maybe she just doesn't like my choice in cravats. Who knows with women?"

Gabriel blinked at him and Evan turned his head so he wouldn't see his younger brother's knowing stare.

"Well, I hope you won't let it interfere with Audrey's wedding," Edward said as he pushed to his feet.

Evan wrinkled his brow. "I would never do that."

"Edward, did you want to go over those figures?" Jude asked, also taking his feet.

Edward laughed and shot Gabriel and Evan a glance. "Three days to his wedding and this one is still managing estate business."

Jude rolled his eyes. "Because I intend to leave you manager-less for several blissful weeks after I make Audrey mine. So take me while you can get me."

Edward clapped an arm around their friend and the two moved toward the door. "So I can't send you messages day and night about estate minutia?" he teased.

"You can, but I won't answer them," Jude chuckled as they left the room.

Once they were gone, Gabriel turned his attention back to Evan. His younger brother leaned back, folding his arms and meeting his gaze evenly. "You haven't really forgotten why Josie hates you, have you?"

Evan glared at him. He had often wished his younger brother hadn't been witness to the afternoon in question.

"I remember something about it," he admitted. "I should have known *you'd* recall it all, with that memory of yours."

Gabriel shrugged. "I pay attention to detail, that's all."

"Yes, you do that," Evan muttered, his own mind recreating the very details he wished he could forget forever. "You know, it was a decade and a half ago. You'd think she could just forget it. I have apologized a dozen times."

His brother lifted both eyebrows. "She must have her reasons. When was the last time you apologized?"

Evan pursed his lips. "The year she came out. So..."

"Eight years ago?" Gabriel said with a shake of his head.

"Well, she hardly spoke to me during those eight years," Evan said, pushing out of his chair and pacing the room. "Even when she was running about with Claire, she'd hardly look at me. Look, the girl doesn't like me. That's fine. She may not even come to Audrey's wedding. Then how she feels or doesn't feel about me won't matter a whit. Hell, if she comes it won't matter. I'll see her for all of a few hours—she'll avoid me. That will be the end of it."

Gabriel shrugged. "Very well, if you say so. Now I am going to go up and talk to Mama for a bit. I'll see you later."

His brother walked from the room and Evan moved back

over to the table. He leaned his hands against the smooth surface and tried to control the tangled emotions that knotted in his chest. Thoughts of Miss Jocelyn Westfall always did that. Damn her.

"This is ridiculous," he barked, then spun from the room and out the front door. He began to make his way down the path to the stable where he would take his horse out for a very long run.

But there was a part of him that knew from bitter experience that he could run his horse into the ground, but he would never fully escape the past. The best he could hope to do was push away the guilt that followed it.

Josie looked up from the stack of papers in her lap as her mother entered the parlor. She smiled and stood to greet Mrs. Westfall with a kiss.

"You look rested," she said.

"Oh yes, I napped the road away very well." Mrs. Westfall laughed as she took her place across from where Josie had been seated and tucked a lock of rich chestnut hair behind her delicate ear.

Josie sighed. Her mother was so very pretty, even in her advancing years. And while Josie had inherited the same color of hair, hers lacked the luster of Mrs. Westfall's. And she certainly did not have the slimness of body her mother had retained even after birthing four children.

"Is that tea?" Mrs. Westfall asked, motioning to the service on the table before them. Josie jolted into action.

"Yes, gracious, I'm sorry. I was woolgathering," she said, pouring the tea into first her mother's cup, then freshening her own. "Would you like a cake?"

"No, I couldn't."

Mrs. Westfall's gaze shifted to the cake on Josie's plate,

sitting half-eaten. She said nothing, but Josie felt her words without needing to hear them. She pushed the plate aside and returned her attention to the paperwork.

"What is that, dear?" Mrs. Westfall asked.

Josie shrugged. "Just a few details here and there about estate things. Some news about the tenant families, that sort of thing. I thought I might make some rounds to them while we're here and asked Charles to gather the information."

Her mother waved her hand. "Oh, Richard should do that."

Josie pursed her lips as she thought of her brother, older than her by more than fifteen years. He wasn't exactly a wastrel, but he liked having money more than responsibility.

"Yes, he should," she said softly. "But since he isn't here, I must take it up in his stead."

She sorted through some of the papers slowly, reviewing staff changes and other minutia with relish. She had always loved facts and figures and reading of any kind. When she glanced up, she found her mother frowning at her.

"You know, someday you'll need spectacles the way you read so much," Mrs. Westfall scolded softly.

Josie forced a smile. "Perhaps you're right."

This was a little game they played. Her mother would half-heartedly try to encourage her to be more focused on her appearance while Josie would pretend to listen. At the heart of it though, she knew the truth. Her entire family had given up on her marrying well years ago. So had Josie, truth be told.

"Is that an invitation in your little pile?" her mother gasped, reaching out to snatch the corner of an envelope that was hidden in the midst of the papers.

Josie laughed. "You are like a bloodhound when it comes to such things!"

Mrs. Westfall glanced up with a smile. "Oh, it is from the Woodleys!"

The smile on Josie's face slipped away and she found herself setting her papers down slowly. "Is it?"

"Yes. I had all but forgotten they were in Briarlake Cross."

"How could you?" Josie teased, trying to lighten the mood for herself. "There was gossip associated with it."

Mrs. Westfall reached out and caught Josie's hands. "Isn't there, though? Lady Woodley's sudden illness? Lady Audrey's whirlwind engagement and upcoming nuptials to Edward's man of affairs?"

"And the grandson of a viscount," Josie added softly.

"Well, of course he is that, so it softens the scandal, but still."

Josie shook her head. Her mother was often an empty-headed gossip, but she was rarely cruel. Even when she was, it wasn't purposeful. She just liked to know about other people.

But Josie knew how damaging gossip and whispers could be.

"And then there is Claire!" Mrs. Westfall continued.

Josie tensed further as thoughts of her friend's desperate situation mobbed her. "Yes, there is no need to mention Claire."

"How can one not when one talks about the Woodleys?" her mother said, waving a hand in front of her face. "I used to be sorry I had a daughter who did not create interest, but then Claire ran away with that scoundrel. Now I am pleased."

Josie shook her head. "Thank you, Mama."

Mrs. Westfall stopped and looked at her, and the color faded from her bright cheeks. "Oh, darling, I'm sorry. That sounded like a judgment and it wasn't meant as one. We are who we are, aren't we?"

"Indeed." Josie sighed as she took the envelope back to look at it. "But instead of rambling on about gossip, why don't we open this note and find out what it says?"

Mrs. Westfall nodded, leaning forward as Josie broke the familiar seal and unfolded the pages.

"It is from Audrey," Josie said. "Welcoming us back to the village, et cetera, et cetera. Ah, well…" She trailed off in her reading, knowing that blood was flooding her face.

"What? What?" Mrs. Westfall all but ripped the pages

back from her and read the last part out loud. "Oh goodness, Audrey is inviting us to her nuptials at the family home in just three days time!"

Josie nodded slowly. "Yes, that is what I read as well," she whispered.

"The whole family will be there," her mother continued. "Oh, how nice it will be to spend time with them again."

Josie squeezed her eyes shut. "Not the whole family."

A frown was Mrs. Westfall's response. "Well, no. Not Claire, of course. But there will be Audrey and Edward, Gabriel and Evan."

Josie pushed to her feet at the mention of Evan's name. She moved to the window and stared out at the garden behind the house. "Of course they will all be there. They wouldn't miss this grand event, would they?"

"You know, we weren't invited to Edward's recent nuptials," her mother said behind her. "We simply cannot miss this set. If we do, we won't be invited to Gabriel or Evan's weddings, for certain."

Josie gripped a fist against the glass. "But perhaps we shouldn't intrude."

She knew her mother would not accept that option, even before she squealed out a sound of derision. "Gracious no! We will go, Josie. I will pen a response right away."

Josie leaned her head forward until the window cooled her suddenly hot brow. "Of course. You know best."

She heard Mrs. Westfall stand and suddenly she was at Josie's elbow. "You know, dearest, in the not-so-distant past, Audrey was on wallflower row with you. And now she is marrying and people even whisper it is for *love*! That should give you hope."

She pressed a quick kiss to Josie's cheek and then flitted out of the parlor, invitation in hand, to pen a response. Once she was gone, Josie rested her arms on the window and her head in her arms.

God, this was a disaster. She didn't want to go to the

Woodley estate. She didn't want to sit and watch Audrey marry and know that Claire, her best friend, her confidante, her sometime protector, wasn't there to see it. She most certainly didn't want to see Evan!

She made a face as she straightened up and returned to the paperwork she had discarded, but she could no longer concentrate as she flipped through the pages. All she could think about was Evan. Evan's cruel words so many years ago and Evan's handsome face that she often found in crowds, sought at parties, the face that followed her into her dreams. An unwanted passenger that always left her confused.

"Damn him," she muttered.

And now she would be attending a family wedding where he would be front and center in the action. There would be no way to avoid him, that was certain. And he would pretend like nothing had ever happened and she would relive her worst childhood nightmares and try to hate him.

What a glorious wedding it would be.

But then again, perhaps he would be so busy with his duties to his sister and Mr. Samson that he wouldn't notice her at all. Her mother spoke of hope. And that was the best Josie could have.

CHAPTER TWO

Josie took a deep breath before she smiled at the Woodleys' butler Vernon and stepped into the foyer.

"Mrs. Westfall, Miss Westfall," he intoned as he took their hats. "The family is expecting you."

"Indeed, they are," came a deep voice from the top of the stairs. Josie closed her eyes tight for a moment, trying to find focus or calm of some sort. But when she opened them and looked up at the man coming down toward her, all that fled.

Evan had always been by far the most handsome of the Woodley clan. In fact, she could easily call him beautiful and not be exaggerating. His dark brown hair was just a touch too long, which gave him a rather disheveled, rakish look even when he was dressed formally, as he was for Audrey's wedding.

He had even darker eyes that had always put her to mind of chocolate. They were bright and always filled with mirth or some mischief. And when he smiled, as he did in this moment, he had a dimple in his right cheek that no other Woodley possessed.

"My lord," her mother said, blessedly interrupting the moment, which allowed Josie to turn her head and compose herself. "How lovely it is to see you. It must be two years!"

"Three," he corrected softly. "Good morning, Mrs. Westfall. Miss Westfall."

Josie refused to meet his welcoming stare and instead examined her slipper. "My lord."

Vernon stepped forward. "I was about to tell the ladies that the family is gathered in the Yellow Room and escort them there."

"You are busy, I know. Go tend to other things," Evan said with a broader smile for the family servant. "I'm happy to make sure the ladies are situated."

The butler nodded with gratitude and scurried away.

"Poor man, he is overwhelmed, as is the entire staff, trying to make my sister's day perfection." Evan laughed. "What they don't realize is that she could be in a potato sack in a field and she would be blissfully happy."

Josie's mother beamed. "So then the rumors are true."

"Rumors?" Evan repeated, his own smile fading slightly. "And what are those?"

"That Lady Audrey has found a love match," Mrs. Westfall continued.

Josie was also interested in that answer, but she refused to show that to Evan, though she leaned a touch closer.

"Indeed," Evan said with a shake of his head. "True love through and through." He tilted his head as he looked at Mrs. Westfall. "You know, my mother has been ill of late. She has not yet joined the rest, but is upstairs with the healer who helped her, Miss Gray, and Jude Samson's own mother, who has joined us in the last few days. I think they would love your company."

Josie jolted. "We wouldn't want to intrude upon—" she began.

But her mother all but shoved her aside. "How lovely."

Evan motioned upstairs. "Turn right at the top of the stairs. It is the third door on the left. It's open and you'll never be lost. They are giggling like a bunch of ninnies."

Josie's mother squeezed her hand and then all but bolted away. Josie watched her go with panic building in her breast. She was about to be alone with Evan Hartwell, the most wicked Woodley of the bunch. And she was not ready.

After all, she had specifically arranged *not* to be alone with him for over fifteen years.

"How are you, Josie?" he asked, breaking into her thoughts.

She frowned at him, mostly because she didn't have a good response when her mind was spinning so. "I'm fine."

He laughed softly, but there was no cruelty to the sound. "Only fine?"

"What answer do you want, my lord?" she whispered.

He shifted at her sharp response, but did not pursue it. "You look very well. That green in your gown is quite fetching."

She looked down at her dress swiftly. She could admit, though only to herself, that she had chosen it on purpose to bring out her eyes. She was far from vain. In fact, she considered her eyes her only good feature. Why not accentuate them?

"Thank you," she said.

At her reticence to expound or make any effort to drive the conversation, he shifted. "Well, I should take you into the parlor with the rest of the family."

At that suggestion, she drew back. "Oh no, I couldn't intrude upon family," she said.

"But—" he began, a strange look on his face that made her feel foolish.

And feeling foolish, especially at this man's hand, made her defensive. "Honestly, why do you argue?" she asked. "I am not like my mother—I know when a day is special enough not to want interlopers."

He held up his hands in surrender. "Fine, I shall take you out to the terrace where the ceremony will be held. There are chairs there for guests."

Josie nodded with relief. Once she joined the rest of the guests, she would be able to excuse Evan and this awful little encounter would end at last.

Except as he guided her through the hallways toward a door that led out onto the wide, stone terrace that wrapped all the way around the manor house, she felt less than eager to see Evan vanish forever.

Why did he have to smell so good?

He pushed the door open and they moved onto the terrace. But instead of being greeted by dozens upon dozens of people from the village and London, Josie was shocked to find not another person there. Just a few chairs arranged before a flower-wrapped wooden arch where Audrey and her intended would soon say their vows.

"What—I—what is going on? Where are the rest of the guests?" she stammered as she spun to face Evan.

He folded his arms. "I tried to tell you that everyone was in the Yellow Room."

She set her jaw. He was being deliberately obnoxious. "You said family was in the Yellow Room."

"Yes." He sighed. "This is a small affair, Josie. Aside from a very select group, the only others in attendance are family." He motioned her to a chair. "But now that we are here, it is actually very nice. Inside they are all talking at once and trying to figure out who will wed next. It's quiet here. So since you insisted on coming out here, I insist on joining you."

Josie's heart sank. Everyone talking at once was perfect for her. She loved that. It meant she could slink against the wall and be forgotten. But out here, with the sun on her face and no one but the one person she didn't want to talk to at her side, she was…exposed.

But since she had demanded this course of action, she could think of no way to escape it and so followed him to the chairs and took the place he motioned to. He sat beside her and closed his eyes, lifting his face to the sun with a long, satisfied sigh.

She took that moment to look at him again. By God, but he had the nicest lips. He was awful. She had to remember that. But that didn't mean she couldn't appreciate his finer qualities.

"So your mother said that Audrey's nuptials are being discussed in London," he said, finally opening his eyes and sliding his dark gaze toward her. "What are they saying?"

"Aside from the part about the love match?" Josie asked. He nodded. "They say that it was a whirlwind."

He arched a brow. "You know what I'm asking. Are they speaking unkindly about her? About Jude?"

Josie shifted. "They—they do call him a servant, though it seems that isn't really true once what he did for your brother is described. And they talk about that his uncle is a viscount but that the family shunned him."

Evan straightened up and those full lips she had been secretly admiring flattened into a hard line. "I see."

"*But*," she continued, "everyone likes Audrey so much that the talk just seems to be matter of fact, rather than cruel."

He shook his head. "That doesn't seem likely."

"Trust me," she whispered. "I know the difference."

He turned toward her and she saw his intention on his face. "Josie—"

"So is it true?" she interrupted, rather rudely she knew, but it didn't matter. She just didn't want to have this conversation with Evan. Not again.

"Is-is what true?" he stammered.

"What they say, what *you* said about Audrey truly finding love? I mean, I'm happy for her if it is. She's lovely and kind and deserving, but just a few months ago, she was half-heartedly pursuing a Season along the wall with me."

Evan pondered that question a moment, then shrugged. "I suppose that sometimes two people can know each other, or think they know each other, for a very long time. Then something happens that changes everything between them."

Josie turned her face. Somehow she didn't want him looking at her when he said those things. "I suppose."

"Josie—" he began again, and again she heard his intention in his voice before he said another word.

"Why did Audrey invite us?" she interrupted.

He jolted slightly. "You have always been so direct," he chuckled.

She shrugged, though heat filled her cheeks. "I only mean that if this day only involves family it seems we are intruders. I wouldn't want to encroach."

He shook his head. "It is silly for you to feel that way," he said. "Josie, you must know why you were invited."

She finally made herself look at him fully. Sitting side by side, their faces were very close together and he was examining her so carefully. Like he was seeing her for the first time.

"Wh-why?" she squeaked out, hating that her voice broke. Hating that she showed Evan anything resembling weakness.

"Because of Claire," he said.

The moment shattered. Here she had been considering how handsome he was and of course the only reason she meant anything to anyone in the Woodley clan was because of her connection to the sister they'd lost.

"Of course," she murmured. "Claire."

He leaned in a fraction closer. "Audrey saw her just a few weeks ago."

Josie tensed. "Hmm," she offered, trying not to commit to saying anything more.

"Have you...have you heard anything from my sister?" he asked.

Josie pushed to her feet and walked away from him, pausing at the edge of the terrace wall to look down below. She didn't want to talk about Claire with anyone. Certainly not with Evan, who she didn't like or trust, despite the fact that she found his face alluring. But she had never been very good at lying. So she stood exactly where she was, hoping that they would be interrupted. Or that the terrace would open beneath her feet and she would disappear.

Evan stared at Josie's trembling back and his heart began to pound faster. He had mentioned Claire as a way to somehow connect to this girl who despised him so completely that she wouldn't even let him apologize again. But now he saw something else in her reticence to answer.

Something more than hatred toward him.

"Josie," he said, rising to his feet and taking a long step toward her. "Do you know something about Claire? Have you heard from her?"

She refused to face him, even when he slid closer. But he saw her tense even more, saw her react to him even when she couldn't see him.

"What are you talking about?" she said, her voice shaking.

He reached for her slowly. "Claire. Your reaction when I said her name was clear. What do you know about—"

"There you are!"

Evan squeezed his eyes shut at the sound of Gabriel's voice coming from the veranda door. When Evan looked, he saw his youngest brother was not alone. He had their mother's arm while Jude followed behind, guiding his own mother. Mary was on the arm of the vicar, and Josie's mother and the healer, Miss Gray, took the final position in their line.

"Oh, Josie darling," his mother said, releasing Gabriel and crossing to her. The dowager folded her into a hug. "It has been too long. I'm so very glad you came. Come and sit with me. Audrey will be down shortly and we will begin."

At last Josie did look at him, but he saw the relief on her face. To be away from him. To keep whatever she knew about Claire to herself. She moved to sit with his mother, her own mother on the other side, and began chatting as the rest of them took their seats and Jude moved to his position at the wooden archway with the vicar.

Behind them, the doors to the house opened and Edward and Audrey came into view. For the moment, Evan forgot Josie's odd behavior and took a sharp breath. His sister was beautiful in her silver gown and fine lace veil. But she had eyes for no one except for Jude at the end of the aisle. She all but floated to him, only acknowledging Edward when he lifted her veil from her face and placed a kiss to her cheek.

The vicar began his ceremony then and Evan found his gaze moving to Josie. She was utterly frustrating, that one. But he somehow hadn't recalled that she was so damned pretty. As a little girl, she had been plump, but the baby fat had melted as she turned into a woman, leaving only lush curves that made her very proper gown seem less so.

And then there was her face. No, Josie was not traditionally pretty like the china dolls who lined up in ballrooms to be called the Diamond of the Season. There was something different to Josie, something...*better*. Maybe it was her heart-shaped face in a sea of fine-boned ovals. Or perhaps it was the bright intelligence to her sparkling green eyes. Then again, Evan could see how one might be enthralled by the tilt to her full lips that hinted at a smile a man could want to coax out, kiss out.

He blinked. What the hell was he doing? This was Jocelyn Westfall he was thinking about! Josie, the annoying childhood friend of his oldest sister. Josie, who couldn't stand him. She wasn't the girl he dreamed about. She was just...*Josie*.

"Mr. and Mrs. Samson!" the vicar said with a smile.

Evan blinked as Jude caught Audrey in his arms and planted a very improper and highly passionate kiss on her lips that inspired both gasps and applause from the friends and family gathered there. Audrey's face was beet red as Jude set her back on her feet and they began to make their way together up the aisle.

As they passed, the dowager got to her feet, dabbing her eyes with a lace handkerchief and said, "We will go to the ballroom for refreshments and be joined there by many friends!"

The family began to stand, stretching their legs and chatting softly as they moved toward the house behind the happy and now very married couple.

"Why do you have such a long face?" Gabriel asked from beside him.

Evan looked at his brother with a frown. "Well, you saw who I was with when you came out."

Gabriel chuckled. "Your nemesis, yes."

"She isn't my nemesis," Evan corrected as the two took up the rear of the line that was weaving its way to the house. "If anything, I seem to be hers. I hardly think of her at all."

Of course, that wasn't true a moment ago, but he wasn't about to share that fact with Gabriel.

"Hmmm." His brother sounded less than convinced. "And did she tell you anything about Claire?"

Evan's eyes went wide. "What? How did you know we were discussing Claire?"

Gabriel shrugged. "When I came out, she wouldn't look at you, she wouldn't look at me, she could hardly even make eye contact with Mama, even while they chatted. The only reason I can deduce for those facts is that she feels a little guilty about something. Hence...Claire."

"God, it is annoying that you can do that," Evan muttered.

"What?"

"Put together all these truths just from a few slim shreds of evidence." He rolled his eyes.

Gabriel thought about that for a long moment. "I suppose I think it must be annoying not to be able to do it. Don't *you* get bored?"

"Only occasionally," Evan said with a meaningful look toward his brother.

Gabriel only laughed. "But what did she say to you?"

"Not much," Evan admitted. "But it doesn't take your deduction skills to guess she has something to hide. One mention of Claire and she jumped out of her seat like I had stuck a tack in her backside."

Her really very perfect backside, now that he saw it twitching up to the double doors ahead of him. A man could really hold on to a set of hips like that. Holding her steady while he—

"What are you going to do about it?" Gabriel asked.

Evan blinked, still distracted by where his entirely errant mind had taken him. He moved into the house and down the hallway toward the ballroom where the families would take up positions in the receiving line and greet the great many people in the village and friends who had traveled for the celebration to come.

"Do about what?"

"Her!" Gabriel said with a snort of frustration. "Great God."

"Why should I do anything about her?" Evan asked, taking his place in the line and dropping his voice so no one would hear. "You should talk to her. She *likes* you."

The moment he said the words, he wished he could take them back. After all, his younger brother was very handsome in his own right and he and Josie had their love of Claire in common. Spending time together could easily lead them to…to something Evan didn't want to consider.

But Gabriel was staring at him like he had grown a second head. "Are you so daft?"

Evan wrinkled his brow. "What? What are you implying?"

Gabriel rolled his eyes with a laugh that drew the attention from several of the young ladies in the line that was forming outside the ballroom.

"I'm afraid she won't say a word to me," his brother said.

The line began to move and suddenly there were hands to shake and felicitations to accept. For a few moments, he and Gabriel did that, and Evan was unable to address the strange statement. But finally one of the villagers stopped at Audrey and Jude's side, holding up the line for enough time that Evan could face Gabriel again.

"Why wouldn't she say anything to you?" he whispered.

His brother shook his head. "Can't you see? Josie Westfall has a *tendre* for you."

"That is patently ridiculous—" Evan began, but Gabriel

cut him off by motioning across the room where Josie was standing with her mother. To Evan's surprise, Josie was staring at *him*. But the moment she caught his gaze on her, she darted her eyes away with a deep frown.

Gabriel laughed. "She hates herself for it, but she does."

CHAPTER THREE

Josie stood on the terrace, letting the cool night air waft over her bare arms, and tried to calm herself. She was failing, failing miserably, and no amount of deep breaths or attempts to clear her mind were working.

It had not been her most stellar of days. After the wedding she'd had the distinct displeasure of post-wedding talk. Her mother had sighed theatrically and lamented how she might never get to plan a wedding.

Even when Josie had pointed out her mother had planned not one but three weddings, two for her older sisters and one for her brother, she would not be consoled. And then there were the rest, kind-meaning people who approached her and asked when *she* would take a husband.

As if she just hadn't thought of plucking one from the crowd of men lining up to wed her.

"The nonexistent crowd of men," she muttered as she looked up at the full moon and tried not to curse it.

When she was honest with herself, the usual conversation about her spinsterhood wasn't what was truly bothering her. It was really her conversation with Evan that made her anxious. She didn't like being with him. It made her feel all odd and hot and not herself. Because she didn't like him.

Except there had been moments when they were sitting together when he'd smiled that she'd sort of...forgotten how much she didn't like him.

"Oh, why can he do that to me?" she snapped, happy to be alone outside so she could berate herself in private. "Why?"

Except she feared she knew why. That little candle she'd burned for him as a girl hadn't ever fully gone out. Even when she hated him with all she was, she'd still found herself watching him. Just like she had all night tonight.

"Idiot. I'm an idiot," she muttered.

The door behind her opened and Josie tensed as she turned to face the intruder. She truly hoped it wasn't her mother or, God forbid, Evan himself. But instead Audrey stepped out into the fresh air and Josie found herself smiling. She had not had the pleasure of more than a few moments of her happy friend's time.

"Are you running away from your wedding?" Josie teased as Audrey came up beside her and took a long breath of air.

She laughed. "Oh, heavens no. I'm far too happy to run. I only needed some air. Do you know that the moment you say 'I do' they then start harassing you about having babies?"

Josie shook her head. "Not being married, nor even close to it, I did not know that."

Audrey glanced at her. "Well, to be fair, until just a few weeks ago I was no closer to marriage than you are now. And a few months before that Edward would have told you he would never wed again. We are proof positive that you *never* know what is going to come around the next corner."

Josie stifled a laugh. "Oh, please don't try to tell me that fairytale that my prince is just waiting for me and I haven't met him yet."

"Perhaps you have met him," Audrey suggested. "You just don't realize he's right there."

Josie suddenly had the oddest image of Evan standing across the ballroom, watching her from the receiving line at the beginning of the night, but she shoved it aside and tried desperately to find a way to change the subject.

"I suppose it makes sense that everyone is pressuring you

to immediately have a child or eight. We are brood mares, after all. Some of them see our only value as providing more people for the Empire."

Audrey's smile went soft. "Luckily that is not what the man I married thinks."

"No, he stares at you like you are a diamond that he must protect," Josie agreed, and heard the unintentionally wistful sound to her voice.

Why did she sound like that? She certainly didn't expect a man like Audrey had found. At twenty-six, the best she could hope for was a man with a bunch of motherless children who was willing to offer her a name or a title in exchange for her help. At the rate she was going, she couldn't even truly expect *that*.

"Yes," Audrey said. "And I do love him, Josie. I know people have talked about our marriage and wondered why everything went so swiftly. The truth is, I love him so completely."

Josie couldn't help but smile at her friend's joy and wrapped her arms around her. "Well, you deserve that, Audrey. You deserve it and a lifetime of happiness producing those eight beautiful children Society demands."

Audrey giggled at her quip and then both women let out a simultaneous sigh.

"I wish Claire were here," Audrey whispered.

Josie nodded. "I was just thinking the same thing."

She almost said more. She almost admitted that she knew Audrey had seen her sister just before her engagement was announced. But that would mean admitting she sometimes heard from Claire. And her friend had made her promise not to do that. Josie kept her promises.

So instead she merely stood there with Audrey, staring up at the moon above, their arms around each other. When a few moments had passed, Audrey stepped away and her sad smile brightened.

"You were my sister's best friend."

Josie shook her head. "No, she had two."

Audrey's face lit up at the words and she swiped at a sudden tear. "Goodness, this will not do."

"Then talk of something else," Josie encouraged as she blinked away her own unexpected tears. "What are your plans now that you are wed?"

Audrey nodded. "London, actually, is next on my list. Jude and I will return to the city with Mary and Edward in the next few days. My brother's gift to us was time off for my husband and a cottage by the sea in the north. So London first and then a glorious, romantic honeymoon that I can hardly wait to start."

Josie blushed at how animated Audrey's face had become. As an avid reader with a father who had hidden some very naughty books before his death, she had some vague understanding of what went on between a woman and a man. Audrey seemed to have a much more detailed one.

"So," she said, grasping on to the less scandalous points of Audrey's statement. "You will all return to London, then?"

In truth, she was relieved. She and her mother intended to spend at least another month rusticating at their small estate on the other side of the village. The fact that Evan wouldn't be there as a distraction was a blessing.

"Oh no!" Audrey said. "Not all of us. Mama is better, thank God, but Miss Gray has made it very clear that she is not to be moved yet. So Evan and Gabriel will stay behind with her."

"Your brother will be here?" Josie said, perhaps a little louder than she had intended to do.

Audrey wrinkled her brow. "Yes, both brothers. Oh, I'm so glad you'll be here. I love Evan and Gabriel, but my mother will be so happy to spend time with you and your mother. And now Jude's mother Hilda has agreed to stay with her as well. She may even take on a permanent place as my mother's companion. Knowing she has so many people visiting and staying with her will make leaving her easier."

"Yes, well, if we're all here in such close proximity we'll come all the time," Josie said, working it out more for herself than anyone else. "All the time. And we'll all see each other. All of us."

Audrey's smile fell. "Are you…are you all right?"

"Of course, why wouldn't I be all right?" Josie asked. "I'm perfect. And I'm so happy for you. You seem so happy."

She was repeating words now, she could hear it. But Audrey was so in love, it didn't seem to fully register. "Thank you, we *are* so happy."

"I'm glad to hear it," came a male voice from the door.

Audrey's smile broadened even before she turned and so when Josie moved to see Jude Samson standing at the terrace entrance, she was not surprised. He was a very handsome man, that was undeniable. He was tall with a rugged face and soulful dark blue eyes. Eyes that seemed to only see Audrey for he never took them off of her. It appeared he loved her as deeply as she loved him.

And that made Josie even happier for her friend, once she pushed past the irrational flare of jealousy that made her blush.

"Mr. Samson," she said, holding out a hand as she moved toward him. "I know we've met a few times before and I already said it tonight, but so many felicitations to you on your…"

She trailed off for as she neared the window that looked into the ballroom she saw Evan in the crowd. Watching them.

"On my?" Samson pressed.

She jolted. "On your marriage, of course. Audrey seems deliriously happy, and we all know she deserves that."

Samson smiled and caught his new wife's hand, drawing her to his side. He looked down on her and Josie blinked at the intimacy of the look they exchanged.

"She deserves that and everything else in the world."

Audrey's lips parted slightly. "All I have ever wanted is right here, I assure you."

Josie turned her face. This was intruding, though to be fair they weren't exactly hiding their passion, their love for each other. And once again that little niggle of jealousy stirred in her belly.

"Did you come out to fetch me?" Audrey asked, blushing as she shot a side glance at Josie.

He nodded. "Lady Kitterage's daughter is to be married at Christmas and she is demanding to know who designed your gown. Your mother is quite engrossed with a few of her guests, and I didn't want to disturb her."

Audrey's eyes went wide at his statement, but then she nodded. "Of course." She turned to Josie with a grin. "Won't she be surprised that it was made by our little country seamstress rather than some fancy London one? I shall enjoy the look on her arrogant face. Will you join me to see it?"

Josie laughed, but shook her head. Lady Kitterage was one of her least favorite people and her nasty daughter had made Josie's life quite miserable over the years. She did not want to see them, even if it meant watching the haughty woman be shocked.

"I am enjoying the air," she said. "But you go. Describe it all to me later."

Audrey hesitated, but then nodded as she took her husband's arm and allowed herself to be led inside. As they left, Josie watched them and let her gaze slip through the window again. Evan was still there. And despite the fact that his sister had come in to join her party, he still watched. Watched her?

No, that couldn't be. Likely he couldn't even see her. He was probably staring off into nothing or planning which biddable widow he would sneak away with for the night.

That thought made her turn away with a huff of breath that was far too telling. It was best she stay outside until she cleared her head. Though at this rate, she could be here all night, perhaps even all week.

Evan folded his arms as he watched through the window. Josie stood at the terrace wall, looking out over the garden. Just as she had been for the half an hour since Audrey and Jude had left her there to return to the party. Now the guests were beginning to slowly make their way out, singing the praises of the new couple and shouting good wishes as they went.

They were down to just a few stragglers when Evan felt a tap on his shoulder. He turned to find Josie's mother, Mrs. Westfall, at his elbow. She stared up at him with a slightly tipsy smile.

"Have you seen my daughter, my lord?" she asked. Evan sighed and slowly motioned outside. Her mother's smile fell. "Oh, that girl!" she ground out.

Evan arched a brow. "I believe she is just getting some air."

Mrs. Westfall shook her head. "Getting some air, my right slipper. She is hiding from the party, just as she always does. How does she ever think she's going to get a husband by mooning about on terraces? I declare, she is trying to send me to Bedlam."

Evan pursed his lips at the barrage and then shrugged. "Well, there she is, whatever her reasons. And I should—"

"Oh, your mama and Mrs. Samson are motioning to me," Mrs. Westfall said. "Would you be a dear boy and go out to tell her we are preparing to depart?" She didn't wait for his response, but patted his arm. "Thank you so much."

Then she spun away and left him still staring at Josie. Irritation built in him, though he didn't exactly know why. After all, Mrs. Westfall had only asked him to do exactly what he'd been pondering for the past thirty minutes: joining Josie in the moonlight.

Now he had a reason.

"As if I need a reason to go out on my own terrace," he

muttered as he moved toward the door. "If anyone needs a reason to trespass, it's *her*."

He pushed the doors open and stepped outside. For a moment, he considered closing them, but decided against it. An open door would discourage...

He wasn't exactly sure what he thought it would discourage. It wasn't as if he intended to sweep *Jocelyn Westfall* into his arms, kiss her until she opened for him, press her against the wall while she begged for him, take her until she trembled.

No. That thought had never crossed his mind. Not even once.

"Josie?" he asked as he neared her.

She jumped at the sound of his voice and spun to face him.

"You scared the devil out of me," she said as she lifted a hand to her breast, all but forcing his gaze to follow. "Why did you sneak up on me?"

He pressed his lips together and forced himself to look at her face and not her gorgeous curves. "I didn't sneak up on anyone," he snapped, his tone as peevish as hers was, though he rather thought for a very different reason.

He had his stupid brother's equally ridiculous words ringing in his head. Words that said that Josie *liked* him. Liked *him*. Which was ridiculous. Josie didn't like him. She hated him.

Even now, she could barely look at him. And when she did with those wide, clear green eyes all he saw was...was...

He blinked as he stared down at her. No, that wasn't hatred in her gaze. Well, perhaps a hint of it, but there was something else there too. Something heated. Something alluring.

Desire. He looked into her eyes and he saw desire there. She was watching his lips, her breath was short, she shifted uncomfortably, but all that was born of the hot and powerful desire that flickered in her stare.

Worse, it inspired an equally heated response in himself.

All those fantasies he had been forcing himself not to visualize came rushing to the surface, and for a moment all he could see was a dozen ways to make her his. A dozen ways to make her quake beneath him, on top of him, around him.

What the hell?

"Your mother is leaving," he snapped, his tone sharp out of confusion and need that would very much go unfulfilled. "She wanted me to fetch you."

His words seemed to break the spell between them and she turned her face. "Good," she muttered, almost more to herself than to him. "It's high time I left."

"W-well," he stammered, holding out his arm awkwardly. "Let me escort you inside."

She shook her head and backed away from his touch. "No, that is entirely unnecessary, my lord. I can very easily find my way myself. Good evening."

She scurried past him without another glance or word and disappeared into the house. Evan forced himself to pivot toward the wall where she had been standing just a moment before. He would not watch her anymore.

Not only because it was pathetic, but because now that he had seen that flicker of wanting in her eyes, he realized that he had to decide what to do about it. And if he wanted to use it to determine what she knew about Claire.

CHAPTER FOUR

Josie sat down at the breakfast table and forced a smile toward her mother. It was returned before Mrs. Westfall said, "Good Lord, you have a shadow beneath your eyes. Are you not sleeping well?"

Josie groaned. Why did her mother have to notice every dratted thing about her?

"A gentleman will notice, my dear," Mrs. Westfall added helpfully.

Josie smiled up at the servant who set a plate before her and then returned her attention to her mother. "What gentleman? We are in the country. Unless you count the man who runs the country store—"

"You hush your mouth," Mrs. Westfall interrupted with a sharp look. "You know I would never mean that."

Now Josie's smile was more real. It was a *little* fun teasing her mother. "Then I'm not certain which gentleman will notice the lack of sleep on my face."

"What about the Woodley men?" her mother pressed.

At the mention of the family title, Josie's appetite vanished on the wind. She had been thinking far too much about just those men—well, one of those men—since Audrey's wedding three days before. Evan had haunted her days and her nights, making her relive every exchange she had been forced to have with him. He was the damned reason for the circles under her eyes, after all.

But her mother didn't know that. Her mother didn't know that she was making everything worse for Josie by bringing *him* up.

Josie set her fork down on the edge of her plate and forced herself not to reveal too much emotion on her face. "Considering Lord Evan and Lord Gabriel are not here and we have not seen their family for three days, I suppose I am not that concerned about it."

Her mother let out a long-suffering sigh. "My darling, you do test me."

"How this time?" Josie asked before she took a long sip of her tea.

"Are you determined to remain a spinster?" her mother asked. "Do you want to live your life alone? Or be forced to remain with me for all of your days?"

"When you aren't haranguing me about the men I must entice into marriage, I rather like remaining with you," Josie said. "Or are you so sick of me?"

Mrs. Westfall shook her head. "I push you. Of course I do. I want to see you settled, as your older siblings are. I want to see you…"

"Married, I know," Josie said to fill the space her mother left unsaid.

"More than that." Mrs. Westfall reached a hand out to cover hers. "I wouldn't mind seeing you happy and taken care of."

Josie blinked at the sudden stinging in her eyes. Her mother could be flighty and gossipy and oh-so-pushy, but there was no doubt her motives were pure.

"But Mama, what if I cannot be happy the way you picture for me?" she asked. "What if my future is not one of a husband and babies?"

"Why?"

Josie shifted. "B-because no one wants me."

Mrs. Westfall shut her eyes tightly. "You were teased as a

girl, ignored. I know it hurt you, but it does not have to guide your entire future."

Josie shrugged. "And you think making some kind of impression on Gabriel or Evan Woodley will change the course of my life?"

Mrs. Westfall stood and walked to the tea service on the sideboard. As she poured, she said, "Well, perhaps not Gabriel. He seems to be interested in that pretty little healer who takes care of his mother. What is her name?"

"Juliet Gray," Josie said as her eyes went wide. "I spent some time with her at the wedding celebration and she is lovely. Does he really like her?"

"He couldn't stop watching her," Mrs. Westfall said with a shrug. "Honestly, that poor family. Between Claire running off with that criminal and Edward's second marriage to a girl who is all but penniless and now Audrey marrying a servant…Susanna must be ripping her hair out."

Josie pursed her lips at the gossipy judgment. "Claire's situation is unfortunate, I'll give you that. But the new Lady Woodley, Mary, is lovely, no matter her origins. And Jude Samson has long been close to the Woodley family. He's the grandson of a viscount at any rate, so you could hardly call him a common servant."

"Perhaps. Still, if you were to align yourself with Evan, there is no way the dowager wouldn't approve."

Josie blinked. In fact, all she could do was blink. "Wait, do you honestly think I am going to match myself with *Evan*?"

"Who else would I mean?"

Now Josie leapt her feet and backed away, as if distancing herself could make that question go away. "You cannot mean that! Not after our past."

Her mother shook her head. "Are you still angry with Evan about that Horsey comment he made fifteen years ago?"

Josie sucked in breath through her teeth. "Because of that comment, every cruel girl and arrogant boy called me Horsey! In public. In private. I heard them mutter it when I walked by.

Sometimes I still hear it! His cruelty inspired over a decade more of it!"

"But he apologized to you," Mrs. Westfall pointed out. "That day. A few times since."

Josie sighed. He had done that, but what good had that done her? His slip of the tongue, his attempt to impress someone mean and awful, had haunted her the rest of her life. He had been able to just walk away from it, untouched and unbothered.

But her mother wouldn't understand that. Her mother had been a Diamond of the First Water, as had both her older sisters. They could never understand the pain and cruelty of being an outcast.

"Even if I didn't have that past with him, trust me that he doesn't like me," she said instead. "The last thing Evan would ever have on his mind when it comes to me is courtship."

"I wouldn't be so sure. He certainly was watching you quite closely at his sister's wedding."

A frown was Josie's first response. Yes, she had found Evan watching her throughout the day, and evening as well. But he had also asked her about Claire and she had stammered in a moment of weakness. It was likely only his interest in her relationship with his missing sister that drove him to seek her out in the crowd.

"Perhaps I had something on my face," she offered instead of the truth.

"Oh, Josie." Her mother frowned. "Whatever you say. But today when you see them, be sure to be polite, at least."

Josie's eyes went wide. "Today? See them? What are you talking about?"

"I was trying to tell you at the beginning before you started arguing with me about your future that we have been invited to spend the afternoon at Briarlake Cross with the remaining Woodleys."

Returning to her abandoned chair, Josie flopped down. She had known this time would come. There was no way that her mother wouldn't arrange to spend time with her friend the dowager, both because the women liked each other and for the attachment to such an important family.

"And why did we not do this sooner?" she asked softly.

Mrs. Westfall shrugged. "Lady Woodley only had a few days remaining with her daughter and son and their new spouses before their foursome returned to London. I wanted to allow her family time. But since the others were to depart this morning, I received an invitation requesting we join them today. I accepted on both our behalves."

"I think I feel a cold coming on," Josie muttered.

"Oh no," her mother said with a hawkish glare. "None of that now. You'll come and you'll have a lovely time and everything will be well."

"While I'm wooing Evan, you mean?" Josie said with a glare of her own.

A laugh was the response. "Just don't rule the man out. He may not be the ogre you have wanted him to be and you are most definitely not the pariah you've made yourself out to be. Give nature a chance to run its course. At least consider it." Mrs. Westfall stood. "And now I have a few things to do before we make our way to Briarlake Cross. Good morning, darling."

Josie halfheartedly returned the goodbye as she stared at her plate. Consider Evan, her mother had said. Consider that he might actually...*like* her? It was a foolish notion, but it tapped into every secret desire she had held before that long ago afternoon when he broke her heart.

And even though she knew her mother was blind to the truth, her suggestion was likely all Josie would consider until she saw Evan again and proved to herself that she meant nothing to him and he nothing to her.

Josie shifted on the settee and tried to look anywhere but

at Evan. It was difficult when there were so few people in the room. Oh, the day had started out benignly enough. When they arrived, Lady Woodley had informed them that Gabriel and Evan were out on a ride around the estate. And though there had been a mild disappointment in that fact that Josie had pushed aside, she had been able to settle into a very nice conversation with Lady Woodley, Mrs. Samson, Miss Gray and her mother.

But as soon as luncheon ended and they had retired to the parlor overlooking the gardens below, Gabriel and Evan had returned and suddenly the room was now filled with masculine energy and Evan's odd stares.

Why did he keep looking at her? And why did he have to be so dratted handsome while he did it? Couldn't he have had a hunchback or crossed eyes or a pockmarked face if she was trying to hate him?

"You have a very faraway look, my dear," Lady Woodley said.

Josie jolted and blushed at being caught with such thoughts in her head. "I'm sorry," she said, searching for an appropriate lie. "I-I was just admiring your gardens."

Lady Woodley nodded. "Are they not lovely? Our staff takes such good care of them and have been bringing in fresh flowers for my room every day of my convalescence."

"You've always had the prettiest roses," Josie's mother said with a sigh.

"They are," Josie said, encouraged by the fact that she caught Evan yawning from the corner of her eye. Perhaps he would grow bored of their conversation and just go away.

"You should take a walk in the conservatory if you like the roses so much, Jocelyn," Lady Woodley said. "The hothouse flowers are also doing very well this year."

"I would love that," Josie said, both because she meant it and because Evan's eyes were glazing over.

"Evan, why don't you escort Josie to the conservatory?" Lady Woodley said.

Josie jolted and turned her full attention to the dowager, even as Evan did the same. "I—" she began.

At the same time, Evan said, "Mother—"

Their eyes locked and Josie folded her arms. Seemed all this talk about him liking her was pure poppycock. He didn't want to walk with her any more than she did with him. And while that should have pleased her, for some reason it did not.

"I think your son would not like to leave you, my lady," Josie said, ice in her tone that she could not control.

Evan's eyes narrowed and for a moment she thought he might defy her words. But he had no chance. Lady Woodley waved her hand. "Oh, ridiculous. I do not need to be handled like I am made of glass. Evan, take our guest. I insist."

Slowly, Evan rose to his feet and held out an arm. "Of course. Miss Westfall, if you would like to come with me, I'm happy to show you the conservatory."

"And take some cuttings if you'd like, my dear," his mother said as Josie got to her feet and stared at the arm outstretched to her.

It was a very muscular arm. And she knew if she touched it, she would be connected physically to this man she had been avoiding for over a decade. Was she ready for that?

She had no choice but to be, because every eye in the room was on them, watching and waiting for her to act politely. And probably wondering why it was taking her so long.

Tensing, she took the arm and tried to ignore the way his muscles flexed as he drew her forward. The way his spicy, male scent filled her nostrils. The way her hand curled perfectly around him, like it was made to go there.

"Take your time, we are having a lovely talk," Josie's mother called out.

She squeezed her eyes shut. There was never any subtly to Rachel Westfall. No one could accuse her of that.

Evan guided her into the hall and down through a maze of twists and turns that led them to a large set of double doors. He released her and she found herself finally able to breathe as he pushed them open and revealed the conservatory.

For a moment, Josie forgot her discomfort, forgot everything except for the beauty before her. The conservatory was a flood of green deliciousness, with trees and flowers and fruits in all directions. She stepped into its steamy heat with a sigh of pleasure and hardly noticed that Evan moved in behind her and shut the door softly.

"It has been years since I was here," she breathed. "We used to play hide-and-seek in this very room. You could be lost forever, I think, and I used to imagine how I would build myself a little house and live off the fruit."

The moment that confession left her lips, she wished she could take it back. She hadn't meant to tell something so intimate to a man she didn't trust. She shot Evan a side glance and found him watching her intently.

"Of course, those were silly, girlish thoughts," she said, trying to distance herself.

"I rather like the idea," he said with a shrug. "You could hide a long time here and not be found if you wanted to."

Josie's retort was on her lips, a quip about why would *he* want to when he had everything he wanted outside those doors. But she held it back. If she were rude to him, it would only drive home the point that she gave a damn. Her best course here was to be calmly polite and hope that would put the distance between them that she so desperately wanted.

"How do you find the weather this summer, my lord?" she asked.

He tilted his head at her question. "The—the weather?" he repeated.

She forced a smile. "Yes. I've found it quite fair. Hardly any rain. Such a refreshing change from last year's torrents all through the summer months."

He was silent for a moment, opening and shutting his mouth like a fish. "Are you—are you making small talk with me? Being polite?"

Josie felt heat flood her cheeks and not just from the effect of the greenhouse. "Yes," she said through gritted teeth. "But you aren't supposed to point it out, you know!"

For a moment, he seemed stunned into silence, but then he surprised her by tilting his head back and laughing. She stared, for he wasn't mocking her. This was real laughter, brought on by their odd situation. And he was so handsome while he did it, the sound of it was so infectious that she found herself doing the same.

He smiled as their shared mirth faded. "I'm sorry, Josie. I didn't mean to so rudely point out your politeness. Will you ever forgive me?"

"This time," she teased back.

But now his expression grew more serious. "Well, that is a start. If you have a small bit of forgiveness in your heart for me, perhaps that means that someday you will have more."

She caught her breath. "I—oh—Evan—" She turned away, ready to bolt, but he reached out and caught her forearm gently.

"Oh, please don't run away. Josie, I don't want us to be enemies."

She swallowed as years of pain came rushing back in a flash. Memories of cruelty, both his unintentional kind and the very intentional kind that had followed.

"Please don't," she whispered.

"Why have you hated me all these years?" he asked, suddenly very close to her. "Was it only that day? I know I was rather silly toward you, but I've seen you be a friend to many. Why can't you forgive me?"

"Silly toward me?" Josie repeated, pulling her arm away from him as she stared up into his handsome and utterly clueless face. "Is that what you think that was? That you were *silly* to me to impress a girl?"

His lips parted. "Yes."

"It was more than that." Her jaw clenched at his utter cluelessness. "You hurt my feelings so very badly. But I could have forgiven that. You threw out a nasty name for me.

Horsey."

"It wasn't intentional," he began. "A slip of the tongue!"

"I don't care," she said back, far more passionately than she meant to. "Don't you understand? That is what everyone called me for years afterward! It has stuck all the way up to now. I was already awkward, I was already plump and unpretty. And you made it all worse because you gave *them* a slur to use when they saw me. And what's worse is that you are staring at me as if I am crazy. You are staring at me as if you hardly remember what was one of the worst days of my life." She turned away from him. "And that is why I have hated you, Evan. That is why your half-hearted apologies have never meant a thing to me."

CHAPTER FIVE

Evan stared at Josie's trembling back, her sharp words like knives in his chest.

"I didn't realize they carried the name forward," he said with a shake of his head. "Why didn't Claire say something?"

"I told her not to," Josie said softly, not turning toward him. "I didn't want to talk to you, to listen to you tell me how sorry you were, to hear the pity in your voice that I hear now. What good would it have done? They still would have called me names—it wouldn't have changed a thing."

"I don't have pity in my voice," he said, moving toward her, wishing she would look at him. "Please, Josie."

She stood stock still for a long moment, then let out a very long sigh and turned to face him at last. Her arms were folded like a shield across her chest, her chin was lifted in defiance and wavering strength, but in her eyes he saw the pain she had suffered. She had never been more beautiful and in that moment he had a strange longing to just...*hold* her.

"I don't feel pity for you," he began. "Because you are not pitiable. The fact that you endured that kind of teasing and are so strong today is a testament to your character. The fact that I participated, even peripherally, in what happened to you is, sadly, a testament to mine."

Her lips parted, but he held up his hand. "Please, let me finish."

She nodded. "All right."

"Jocelyn Westfall, I did you a wrong. And I am truly sorry. Not half-heartedly, but truly. And I hope that you can forgive me at last."

She was looking at his face, exploring it like she could determine if he was being true. He hoped he could see that he was. His odd desire for her and the fact that he thought she might know something about Claire aside, he did want to make up for what he'd done.

"I can accept your apology," she said at last.

He frowned. She said the words, but there was still hesitation in her eyes, in her voice. Perhaps that was born after years of habit when it came to mistrusting him, but he thought there was more to it.

"Who was the girl?" he asked.

She blinked in confusion. "The girl?"

He nodded. "You said that I was trying to impress a girl. I vaguely recall her, but who was it?"

Josie shook her head. "Viscount Aldridge's eldest daughter, Aurora. I think she's Lady Denham now."

Evan recoiled. "*That* girl?" He shuddered. "God, she must be the biggest bit—" He cut himself off. "She is one of the nastiest women in Society. I thought her attractive?"

"She was very pretty," Josie admitted, he thought reluctantly. "She still is. She and her younger sister Philippa made great sport about teasing me." She bit her lip. "Occasionally they still do when they feel they can get away with it."

Evan clenched his hands at his sides at the thought that Josie was still being tormented. "How about this? I will make it up to you."

"How?" she asked, incredulous tone proving she had no trust for him whatsoever.

"When we return to London, I will give those little witches the cut direct. I will make it clear to all that no one will get away with calling you names again."

She tilted her head with a small laugh. "And how will you

enforce that edict, Evan? It isn't as if we will be together all the time."

Evan hesitated. The idea of being with Josie all the time was not as unpleasant as it should have been. He could almost see it perfectly in his mind. Dancing with her at midnight, stealing a kiss, taking her home to his bed.

He shook his head. "We'll work it out."

"It doesn't matter," she began, moving to turn away again.

He caught her arm, tugging her a bit closer, not allowing her to turn her back to him and shut him away. "But it does," he said softly. "I see how much it does now."

Her tongue darted out to wet her lips as she stared up at him, and something dark and deep stirred in him. That desire he didn't want to feel roared back to the surface, tormenting him.

"I appreciate that," she whispered, her gaze suddenly back on his lips as it had been a few nights before.

"I really am sorry that my words helped in any way to make your life hell," he whispered.

She smiled. "I believe that, perhaps for the first time. But you know, it wasn't always awful. I had Claire. Claire made it sweet enough times that the bitter didn't destroy me."

He tensed. Here was Josie, opening up to him in a way that meant she was beginning to forgive him, and yet she was also giving him an opening to press her about Claire. He could use this moment to get what he wanted. And yet, that felt so...terrible.

But it was Claire! And perhaps something Josie revealed in her weakness could help their family.

"You loved Claire, I know. You were like a second sister to her," he said.

"My own sisters were so much older, I hardly even existed for them. I honestly still don't. So Claire was truly my sister in every real sense of the word."

"You must miss her as deeply as we all do," he whispered.

"I do," she admitted, but he noticed her gaze flitted away.

Slowly, he slipped a finger beneath her chin. Her skin was so soft under his rough fingertip he suddenly wanted to stroke her all over. She tilted her face up.

"Do you ever hear from her?" he asked.

She caught her breath, though he wasn't certain if it was from the unexpected intimacy of the moment between them or from his question. Perhaps both.

"Do you know something?" he pressed, but he found his lips descending toward hers. Lower, lower, and then he kissed her.

He hadn't meant to kiss her at all. But now that he was doing it, it felt more right than any other kiss he'd had in years. Her lips were as soft as her skin and he melted against them, lifting his hands to tilt her face, brushing his lips back and forth against her as he coaxed her to open, to welcome.

And to his surprise, she did. Her lips parted on a sigh and he darted his tongue inside, tasting the sweetness of her like a man starved for far too long. Once he had, he couldn't let go. He molded her closer, sucking her tongue and drawing her in until she felt like a part of him.

And she did not resist. In fact, her hands came up to his upper arms, fingers digging into him through his clothes as she lifted to meet him. Slowly, she became more daring, swirling her own tongue against his, exploring his mouth with hesitance that gently blossomed into passion.

But just as swiftly and powerfully as the kiss began, it ended. With a cry, she pulled herself from his arms and spiraled away, nearly tripping into the flowerbeds neither one of them had spent any time exploring.

"Josie," he began.

"Don't," she whispered, her voice broken. "Oh please, don't!"

Then she gathered her skirt into her hand and ran.

Josie paced the first room she had come to after fleeing the conservatory. The billiard room was vast and masculine, but she didn't give a damn. Her mind was very much elsewhere.

"What did you do?" she gasped out loud. "Oh God, what did you do?"

But she knew what she'd done. She'd allowed Evan to kiss her. She'd very much kissed him back. And now as she thought of it, her errant mind took her back to the moment and she felt as much of a thrill and desire as she had then.

But with Evan? Evan whom she had an infatuation with since she was a girl? Evan whom she had vowed to despise the rest of her days? Why in the world had she had to kiss Evan?

"Josie."

She froze in her pacing at the sound of Evan's voice at the door behind her. She refused to look at him. Looking at him wasn't going to help.

"How did you know I was here?" she whispered.

"I followed you," came his voice again, after a brief hesitation.

She squeezed her eyes shut. "Please Evan, go away. Just go away and let's pretend the conservatory never happened."

She heard him move and she forced herself to look at him, if only to ensure that he wouldn't intrude upon her space again and prove to them both how weak she was. He had shut the door and they were alone. In a dim billiard room.

Alone.

Her breath caught.

"Josie, please," he began.

She shook her spinning head. She couldn't let him talk her into anything. Because he would. With his dark brown eyes, and his full lips, he would spin some kind of spell on her, just like he had in the orangery. She would forget herself if she didn't find a way to distance them.

But her mind was too addled to concoct some lie. And she found herself instead blurting out the truth.

"I know no one is going to marry me!"

The moment she said the words, she wished she could take them back. They sounded so pathetic.

"What?" Evan asked, his brow wrinkling and his face confused.

"Oh God," she said as she spun away and moved across the room again. Maybe distance would help. Certainly standing so close to him did nothing to clear her addled mind.

"What do you mean by that?" he pressed, and to her surprise and horror and a bit of relief, he moved on her again.

She swallowed. "I-I know my situation better than anyone. No one wants me, no one ever has. So I don't expect to marry. I'm not even sad about that fact."

Well, that wasn't entirely true. Sometimes she thought about her life in the future, alone and it did make her sad. But then she thought about independence and it helped a little.

"And this has to do with you running because...?" Evan asked, dragging out the last word into a long question.

She folded her arms.

"I-I suppose I'm just confused by this between us," she admitted, motioning her hand back and forth between them.

He smiled slightly and her heart thumped. Why, oh, why did his smile have to be crooked? Why, oh, why was she so stupidly attracted to him even after everything that had happened between them?

"Confused by what?" he pressed, and he moved closer again. Now she was just a foot away from him and she swore she could smell the heated, leathery scent of him. She felt a strange throb between her legs and squeezed her thighs together to make it stop.

It didn't stop.

"By...by...I don't know," she whispered. She could hardly breathe as he moved forward again and reached out his hand. She watched it cup her cheek in slow motion.

"By this?" he whispered, and his lips dropped her hers again.

She should have pulled away, pushed away, screamed,

slapped him, but none of those were her reaction. Instead she found herself lifting into the kiss, opening her mouth for the wicked, hot invasion of his rough tongue. He tasted ever so faintly of sugar and whiskey, and that combination made her head spin.

She felt like she was getting swept away on a heady sea, and that at some point she wouldn't be able to return. But there was a part of her rational mind that screamed at her to fight the riptide before it was too late.

She pulled back and broke the kiss, but couldn't manage the strength to extract herself from his arms, which had somehow came around her as he kissed her. And in those strong arms, she felt...safe.

A foolish lie.

"Yes," she whispered. "*That*. That is what confuses me. I just don't understand."

He lifted his eyebrows. "Do you need to?"

She pursed her lips. When it had become clear that she was not going to be a great beauty and that she would be teased mercilessly by some of her peers, she had retreated into the world of books. Learning the answers to questions had been one of her most favorite pastimes. And now Evan asked if she needed to understand this most base of her desires?

"Yes," she said. Then she shook her head. "No? Yes."

He smiled at her swinging pendulum of answers, but she didn't feel like he was making fun of her. He released her from his embrace and she felt both relieved and bereft. But he caught her hand instead and stroked his thumb along the webbing between her thumb and forefinger. She almost stopped breathing.

"You aren't alone," he said. "I assure you, this connection, this desire to touch you, it is confusing to me too. After all, you have been my strongest critic, my most vocal enemy for over a decade."

Josie shifted. When he said it that way, she sounded quite petulant. Perhaps she had been in some ways, though he had deserved some of her ire, *that* she knew.

"But," he continued, lifting her hand to his chest, "is it wrong to simply follow what we want?"

Josie blinked. "What exactly are you offering me?"

He locked stares with her and she felt the world beginning to spin again. "What exactly do you want? Right now I'd give you anything."

Her lips parted and he took the opportunity she hadn't fully meant to give. His mouth covered hers and she was lost once more. She wrapped her arms around his neck, shivering as she slid his hands to her waist and molded even closer to her. It was so intimate, and with someone she swore she wanted no conversation with, let alone *this*.

And yet there was no way to resist it. This was attraction, plain and simple, something she couldn't control. He stroked her tongue with his and her body grew hot and liquid. For the first time, she understood how Claire could be swept away by a dangerous man with only pretty whispers and sweet kisses to recommend him.

Her eyes flew open at that thought. Claire had been swept away by passion. Dangerous passion just like this one. And she had paid the price.

With a groan of pain, she pushed away from Evan and shook her head. "No, no I can't. I-I must go now. Please don't follow me. Please."

He opened his mouth to say more, but she refused to allow it when she knew his seductive words would only draw her back into his web. She walked away and this time he did not follow.

Evan was still standing in the billiard room nearly an hour after Josie left him a second time. And although his mind was filled with wild thoughts, he had made no sense out of what had transpired between them.

He hadn't meant to kiss her. Or chase her. Or corner her. Or kiss her again. He certainly had never had the intention of *wanting* her. Her? Josie Westfall? Never.

Except that he did. Even now he could feel her soft, full curves pressed against his body and he went hard at the memory. How he wished he had just thrown caution and shared history and gentlemanliness out the window and laid her across the billiards table. He could have made her come in few moments, he could have tasted her, claimed her.

"And then where would you be?" he snapped out loud as a way to wake himself from his odd daydream. "Shackled to Josie?"

The door behind him opened and Gabriel strode into the room. His brother's face was drawn down in a deep scowl and his brows were furrowed together in the same look that all the Woodley clan shared when frustrated.

"Gabriel," Evan said.

His brother blinked, as if he had been unaware of Evan's presence until his name was said. "Oh, yes, hello."

"Were you looking for me?" Evan asked.

Gabriel shook his head. "No. No. I don't know. I suppose I wondered where you went off to when Josie came back to the parlor alone."

Evan tensed at the mention of her name. "Are *they* still here?"

"Josie and her mother? No, Josie claimed a headache and they went home just a short while ago."

"Then why do you look so troubled? Only Josie Westfall could inspire such frustration as far as I'm concerned."

His brother stared at him like he had grown a second head. "Trust I hardly think of Josie—she could not upset a flea. No, I just had a conversation with Juliet about Mama."

Evan blinked as he tried to place who in the world Juliet was. And then it came to him. He tilted his head. "Miss Gray? The healer?"

"Yes, that's what I said," Gabriel snapped.

Any curiosity Evan might have had about that statement was replaced with tense concern. "Is Mama all right? Is something wrong?"

"No," Gabriel ground out. "Mama is fine. It was a simple disagreement, that is all."

"You had a disagreement with—"

Gabriel cut him off with a wave of his hand. "What about Josie, though?"

"What about Josie?" Evan asked, tension tightening in his chest.

"Did you discover something?" Gabriel pushed as he moved to the sidebar and poured himself a drink.

Evan let out a long breath. Oh, he had discovered a great deal. Like how Josie felt like heaven. Or tasted like ripe peaches. He had discovered that all the discord between them certainly translated into a passion unlike any he'd ever felt for a woman.

But he doubted Gabriel meant that when he spoke of discovery.

"What exactly did you think I would discover?"

Gabriel rolled his eyes. "You spent a great deal of time alone with Josie today. Didn't you think to ask about Claire?"

Evan pursed his lips. That was how all this had begun, wasn't it? He had thought Josie knew something about Claire and he'd been willing to roam into the lion's den to discover what. But once he had made it past Josie's barriers, Claire had somehow become secondary. He'd seen Josie's pain, he'd felt her desire, he'd been lost in her.

His sister be damned.

"I-I did ask about her," he admitted.

Gabriel leaned closer, his dark eyes growing bright and focused. "What did Josie say exactly?"

Evan hesitated. Gabriel was such a stickler for details. His brother would analyze them relentlessly to souse out any tiny thread. It was one of his greatest skills, but at the moment Evan didn't want Gabriel to turn his expertise on him. What had happened between him and Josie was far too…private. And very confusing.

"The topic of Claire came up, but only peripherally," he said. "Josie is cagey when it comes to our sister."

"That isn't exact," Gabriel said with an arch of his brow.

"I wasn't recording our conversation with an eye for repeating it back to you," Evan snapped, throwing up his hands. "God, you will drive a man to madness."

Gabriel shook his head. "You too. Fine, so you don't know exactly what was said. But we can still work with the fact that she wants to avoid the subject of Claire entirely. How did she do that?"

Evan held back a laugh. Oh, they had certainly found a way to avoid the topic. He wasn't going to tell his brother that.

"She, er, ran," he admitted.

Gabriel drew back. "Interesting. And what did you do?"

"Followed her here to the billiard room." He shifted. "But the topic didn't come up again."

"And then she returned to the parlor and almost immediately told her mother she had a headache to further escape." Gabriel set his drink down. "She definitely knows something. And she's obviously close to telling you. You know what you must do, don't you?"

Evan shook his head. He had a sneaking suspicion he knew exactly what his brother would say. "Get closer to her?"

"Get closer to her," Gabriel repeated. "Push harder."

Evan jolted. Oh he wanted to push harder, all right. He wanted to push past all of Josie's barriers until she was his. And that twisted want was like a fire in him that he couldn't quench.

"I'm not sure that's a good idea," he whispered.

"Why?"

"It seems unkind to play upon whatever lingers between us," he said, thinking of the pain in Josie's eyes when she'd confessed to how much he'd hurt her. How much so many people had hurt her.

"Don't you want to save Claire?" Gabriel asked.

Evan looked at his brother. Gabriel and Claire were twins and their connection had always run deep. Now he saw his brother's deep pain, his panic, his need to save her. And that touched him as powerfully as anything Josie had whispered in the conservatory.

And then there was Claire, out there with a villain having God knew what done to her. Evan tried not to picture what her life was like, but sometimes it haunted him.

"Yes," he said softly. "I want to save her. But I don't want to hurt someone she loves in the process. Claire would never forgive me."

"Then don't!" Gabriel cried out with a frustrated shake of his head. "I've watched you in action for years, Evan. There is no one more well versed in the female form than you. You know the line between flirtation and something more serious."

"Do I?" Evan asked, thinking of all those passionate kisses and just how close he'd come to making them something more. "It sometimes seems I don't."

Gabriel caught his arm and shook it. "Please, just keep working on Josie, will you? For me? For Claire?"

Evan let out a long sigh. He couldn't deny his family. So he nodded. "All right. I'll keep working on her."

His brother smiled and the look of relief on his face moved Evan. But it also made him think of Josie. Of all the damage he could do to her, to them both, if he couldn't walk the very fragile line between her desire and her hate.

CHAPTER SIX

Josie shifted the basket on her arm and waved to her maid as Nell exited Martin's general store with a bottle in her hand.

"Here it is, miss! The very last one!"

"Oh, thank you, Nell. I'm sorry, I would have gone and collected it myself, but you know how Mrs. Swanson can talk the ear off a goat. I could not escape her easily."

Nell laughed. "That she can, but it weren't no trouble. Mr. Martin said he'd put the cordial on your account."

Nell let out a huge sneeze at the end of her statement and shook her head with a look of pursed-lipped frustration.

"Bless you! And Mrs. Howard will love it, I know," Josie said as she placed the bottle carefully in her already full basket. There was bread and other pastry in there, seeds from their very own garden, a salve, several pairs of socks, a salami and now the bottle of cordial, along with a few other sundries.

"Please tell me you two are going on the oddest picnic in the history of Britain."

Josie froze in her place as the all-too-familiar voice washed over her. She didn't want to look. She couldn't look. She ought not look.

And yet...she still turned and faced Evan. She had not seen him in nearly three days, not since their heated, odd, wonderful encounter in the billiard room. It had been all she thought about since, but she managed to remain calm as she said, "Good afternoon, my lord."

He arched a brow at her formality, but continued to grin at her. "Good afternoon, Josie and…"

"Nell, my lord," her maid said with a glance between Josie and Evan. She stifled yet another sneeze.

Josie gritted her teeth. Some girls told tales to their maids about gentlemen. But as much as she liked Nell, she hadn't said a peep about what had happened between Evan and her.

"And Nell," Evan said with an acknowledging nod. "Now, do tell me, you two have a very mixed basket there. What *are* you doing?"

Josie wished she could fold her arms, but with the basket in the way, it was impossible. So she made her tone very frosty as she said, "Well, if you must know, Nell and I are about to make the rounds of those who live and work on my late father's lands."

Evan's smile fell a little, replaced by an expression of surprise. "You are?"

"Yes. I do it every time I come here for any extended period," she explained. "My mother usually goes with me, but today she is actually with *your* mother. So Nell is going to accompany me."

The maid responded with another sneeze.

"Gracious, are you all right?" Evan asked, his focused attention suddenly shifting to the maid.

Nell just stared up at him, smiling slightly. Josie rolled her eyes. Trust Nell to be taken in by a handsome face. A very handsome face with the most kissable dimple.

Damn, now she was doing it.

"The horse chestnut tree seems to make Nell sneeze," Josie explained. "In London we don't have any, but here we are in the country."

"I'm perfectly fine otherwise," Nell said, then let out a sneeze that belied her statement. "Thank you for inquiring, my lord."

Evan shook his head. "If you are going out to see the tenants, you're going to be strolling right through copses of the trees. You will explode."

"I have a handkerchief," Nell offered weakly.

Evan folded his arms. "It will not do. No, Nell, you will march back home right away and have a good hot tea."

Josie stepped forward. "Now wait just a moment, you have no right to tell my servant what to do."

"Do you want her to sneeze all day? It sounds painful," Evan asked. He had a smile on his face, damn him, for he knew she wouldn't agree that Nell should hurt herself.

"Of course not," Josie sighed. "Come, Nell, we should go back. I'll see if someone else can accompany me. Or wait for my mother and go tomorrow."

"No, no," Evan said, swooping in to gently remove the basket from her arm. "This is beastly heavy, Josie, great God."

"What are you doing?" Josie asked, ignoring his comments and grimaces about the basket.

"*I'm* going to accompany you," he said, blinking at her as if that should have been perfectly clear. "Go on, Nell, your mistress is perfectly safe with me."

"No one is perfectly safe with you," Josie muttered and to her surprise Evan laughed. She frowned at him and turned to Nell. Her maid shifted with discomfort.

"I don't know, miss. Is that proper?"

Josie glared at Evan, but then shrugged. "Not precisely, I suppose. But Evan is an old friend to our family and his brother is the marquis, so in truth, all our tenants are also under Lord Woodley's charge. And Evan is right, you are going to suffer all day. I should have been more mindful of that fact and I apologize for my lack of care toward you."

Nell waved her hand. "My reaction has never been so strong."

"Go back, have tea and do not worry yourself," Josie said, well aware that Evan was watching her every move. She rather wanted to slap him for it, actually. Or kiss him again. She would choose to do neither, though the second was so very tempting.

Relief flooded Nell's features. "Oh, thank you, miss. And thank you, my lord."

Nell scurried away and Josie took a long breath before she turned back to Evan. "What do you want with seeing tenants with me?"

He laughed. "You said it yourself that the charges of your father are also in some ways the charges of my family."

"Well, all your *charges* got a good dose of Woodley wisdom and company while your brother and his wife were here. They visited every single person in the shire."

Evan blinked. "Edward and Mary did? I thought they went out for just a long ride."

Josie turned her eyes upward with a sigh. "Evan."

He moved a little closer. "Please don't say my name like it's a curse."

She jerked her gaze toward him. His tone was teasing but his eyes were serious.

"I'm sorry," she said softly. "Old habits, you know."

"We should form some new habits," he returned, his voice silky.

She shivered despite herself and didn't resist when he took her arm and led her across the main street to the phaeton that was parked there.

"Oh," Josie said with surprise. "Nell and I were going to walk."

"Don't you like phaetons?" he asked as he set her basket in the tiny space behind their seat and then helped her up.

She wobbled slightly in the high perch. "I-I don't think I've ever ridden in one. My mother doesn't own one and it isn't as if I get invited to ride by the kind of fast gentlemen who do."

Evan laughed again as he took a place beside her and urged the horses forward. "Well, consider yourself in the company of a fast gentleman."

"I do," she muttered under her breath, but his chuckle told her that he had heard her yet again.

And in truth, she rather liked that he laughed at her little quips. In London, there were gentlemen who looked at her like she was speaking another language if she made a sarcastic remark. Certainly her intellect and wit had done her no favors in the marriage mart.

Which was part of why the fact that she would likely never marry didn't trouble her. Much.

"My mother will likely give me a full report tonight," Josie said, searching for a comfortable topic. "But how is Lady Woodley's recovering going?"

"Very well, actually. Ever since Mary suggested the healer. Mary—that is Edward's new wife, you know, who I think you would adore."

"I've heard nothing but good about her. We talked briefly at Audrey's wedding and I did very much like her. She is not at all like Alice."

Both of them shuddered at once. "No," Evan agreed. "Edward's second wife is nothing like his first. And *that* is all the more to recommend Mary to us."

"Tell me more about the healer," Josie said. "She is very pretty."

"Is she?" Evan said, his gaze darting to her in what seemed like true surprise.

Josie shook her head. "Oh, please. It is an undeniable fact that Miss Gray is lovely. I'm surprised you haven't found your way to cornering *her* in the billiard room."

The moment she said those words, she wished she could take them back. First, they brought up a subject she was trying to ignore, but also because she now wondered if Evan, indeed, had done that already with the pretty, auburn-haired healer. Josie couldn't possibly be special in that regard.

Evan turned her to with a frown. "I'm not exactly in the habit of doing that, Josie. Certainly I have no interest in doing it with Miss Gray."

"Oh," Josie said, both embarrassed and secretly pleased with his answer. "Well, at any rate, I was just saying she was pretty and wondering what you thought of her."

"She seems a nice enough girl, though for all the time she spends in our home with our mother, she speaks mainly to Gabriel, rather than me. And she saved our mother's life, so we must all like her."

"Was it truly so dire?" Josie whispered, trying to picture her own life without her mother. She would really have no one at that point, since she wasn't close to her siblings. Oh, one of them would take her in, she supposed. But it wouldn't be out of love, but duty.

"Very," Evan said, all humor gone from his voice. "When we first arrived from London, I think she was on death's door. It was...horrifying."

Josie reached out and covered his hand with hers. His gaze slipped down to her hand before he looked at her face, and she caught her breath. He wanted to kiss her. She recognized it now, that heavy-lidded expression.

Worse, she wanted him to do it.

But he didn't. Instead, he moved to stare straight ahead, his jaw set, and said, "But we've talked about my family more than enough. How is yours?"

Josie pulled her hand back to her lap. It seemed for all his smiles and teases that perhaps Evan regretted what had happened between them. She pushed aside her hurt at that fact.

"Oh, you know. My brother is so busy running everything that he hardly ever calls on us. My sisters are married, with their children and their charities. I suppose they're all well enough."

"You were never close to them," Evan said, a statement not a question.

She shook her head. "No. But they were all so much older. Lydia is the youngest after me, and she is fifteen years older than I am. What could we possibly have in common? I was a surprise youngest child who only served to split the family inheritance further. Why would they *want* to be close to me?"

Evan frowned. "When Edward was estranged from our family after his first wife's death, it was terrible. I suppose I have a hard time picturing not being a friend to my siblings."

"But your family is wonderful," Josie explained, smiling as she thought of the days she had spent in their company. "Aside from you, I loved spending time with all of them."

He laughed, and she blushed as she realized what she'd just said to him.

"I didn't mean—" she began.

"I know what you meant," he reassured her. "You had a history with me that made it hard to want to be my friend, but with Edward or Gabriel or Audrey or especially Claire, you were welcomed."

She nodded. "Yes. I felt a part of that circle when I truly needed to be a part of something."

"Mostly thanks to Claire I would wager since we boys were rather busy being hellions and Audrey was so much younger," he pressed.

She squeezed her eyes shut. "Yes, Claire was my angel so many times. Without her, I can't imagine what my childhood would have been like, let alone those awful first few years of my debut."

For a moment, Evan was silent and shifted beside her in what seemed like discomfort. Then he said, "Do you ever wonder what she suffers now?"

He had brought up the subject of Claire before, and Josie had avoided the subject as much as she could. He was trying to ascertain if Claire had written to her, that much was clear. Josie slid her gaze to his face. His mouth was drawn down and his pain was palpable.

"Evan," she said softly. "I know you all fear for her. You want her safe return. But…"

She trailed off and he set his jaw. "What do you know?"

She sighed. Of course he would press her on this subject. This one subject she couldn't discuss. After all, what little Claire had shared with her was private. Knowing it would give Evan no pleasure.

"When Claire is ready to come home, I have to believe she

will." Up ahead she saw a little cottage at the turn in the road and breathed a sigh of relief. "Ah, and here is our first stop."

Evan continued to frown as he brought the horses to a halt. As he got down and came around the phaeton to help her down, she took a long breath. This day with Evan was unexpected, but as long as they could stay away from difficult subjects and she didn't make a cake of herself…well, at least she could try to enjoy herself.

Evan watched Josie as she stirred a pot of steaming liquid and smiled at the older woman at the worn kitchen table.

"Mrs. Howard, this sauce smells divine," Josie said. "Now, what should I add next?"

"You really shouldn't, my dear," Mrs. Howard fretted as she smoothed her palms along her well-worn skirts.

"But I insist! I never get a chance to play in the kitchen at home. Cook would have a spell." Josie laughed. "Shall I add the herbs we chopped earlier?"

"Yes," Mrs. Howard said. "Then just put the lid on and we'll let it simmer a while."

Josie did as she had been asked, smiling and chatting and asking about Mrs. Howard's children all the while. Evan leaned back to enjoy the show.

He had chosen to horn in on Josie's day out for two reasons. First, he was under strict orders from Gabriel to obtain information about Claire. That had been a failure, for Josie steered him away from the subject every time he tried to broach it.

The other reason was because he found himself *wanting* to spend time with her. In that aspect, the day had been a smashing success. Whether it was in his phaeton, rushing around corners just a little too fast so that she squealed in delight, or spending time with her family's tenants, he had truly enjoyed the afternoon.

And he was beginning to see just how much he had underestimated Josie. At parties she was quiet, the dull bluestocking in the corner. But here her face was full of animation and life and kindness. Her smile was bright and true. And she was absolutely gorgeous.

"Thank you for taking time out of your trip here to call, Miss Westfall," Mrs. Howard said as Josie rejoined her on the settee. "I am so sorry to miss your mother."

"Oh, I'm certain Mother will say her hellos another day," Josie reassured her with another of those kind smiles. "I couldn't miss my chance, though. I do so love calling on everyone and hearing the news."

Evan smiled softly. From some women of Josie's station, those words would be condescending. From her, they were very real. *She* was very real.

"And to bring Lord Evan." Mrs. Howard shot him a shy glance. "If I'd known, I would have dressed better."

"You are lovely," Evan assured her with a quick wink for Josie.

"Oh, I almost forgot!" Josie leapt to her feet and scurried to the basket that Evan had set by the door after their entry nearly an hour before. "You are my last stop of the day and I couldn't come empty-handed."

She held out the bottle and Mrs. Howard's eyes went wide. "Cordial!" she cried, taking the offering.

Josie nodded. "Indeed, to make up for all of it I drank over the years when I came calling with my mother and father. I know it isn't as fine as yours."

"Oh, I haven't made mine for so long, but I do adore it," Mrs. Howard laughed. "This brings back such happy memories."

"Well, share it with your grandchildren when next they call, and think of me," Josie said, patting the older woman's hand. She glanced back at the window. "Oh goodness, the afternoon is flying by. I suppose we should go."

Evan got to his feet. "We should, indeed, if I am to return you to your mother before she believes you've been abducted by gypsies."

Josie helped Mrs. Howard to her feet and the two women linked arms as Evan led them from the modest cottage. Once outside, Josie squeezed Mrs. Howard's hand. "Thank you again for your kind hospitality."

Mrs. Howard smiled before she leaned up and whispered something in Josie's ear. Josie blushed. "Er, yes. Thank you. Goodbye!"

Evan held out a hand and he saw a flicker of both desire and hesitation in Josie's eyes as she took it. The spark between them flared as they touched, but the moment she was safely in the high vehicle, she released him, the flame on her cheeks still bright.

"Goodbye," he said to Mrs. Howard before he climbed up and nickered for the horses to ride on. "What did she say to you?" he asked, watching Josie from the corner of his eye as he urged the horses off the main street and down a little side road.

Josie shook her head. "Oh, it was nothing."

"Liar, liar," he taunted softly.

She glared at him. "She just made some comment about your being my...my beau. Which is, of course, patently ridiculous."

"Is it?" he asked, driving them through a tree-lined lane that twisted and turned toward the water in the distance. So far Josie hadn't seemed to notice their destination. She was too busy picking at her sleeve and trying to avoid eye contact with him.

"Of course," she whispered. "You are...you. And I'm me."

"And?"

"And it's just...silly."

"Then why am I stopping at the edge of the lake so I can walk with you in private instead of taking you home like an uninterested party would?" he asked.

Her head jerked up and she stared as he brought the horses to a stop. "I—what—Evan?"

He laughed. "A valid argument if ever I heard one."

She shook her head. "What are you doing?"

"I think I just said what I'm doing," he said as he climbed down and came around to her side of the rig. He held up a hand, but she just stared.

"Why?" she asked.

He blinked. No woman had ever questioned his motives for pursuit before. But then again, Josie was unlike anyone he'd ever known.

"Because I've spent the day realizing just how irresistible you are, Jocelyn Westfall. And I don't want it to end."

"Oh," she whispered. There was another moment of hesitation, then she took his hand and let him help her down from the rig.

He slipped her hand into the crook of his arm and they began to walk toward the lake. He took a side glance at her.

"What did you mean when you said I was me?"

She shrugged. "You know."

"No, I truly don't."

She worried her lip with her teeth before said. "I suppose I mean that you are Evan of the Woodley clan, *Lord* Evan. Son of a marquis, brother of a marquis! Beyond that, perhaps a little *because* of that, you are popular and well-liked and beautiful."

He smiled slightly at the last word, but didn't address it. "And why is that different from you being you?"

"I was a fat, unattractive girl who everyone made fun of," she said, a little bitterness in her tone. "And even when I stopped being so very plump, I'm a boring bluestocking who prefers books over people any day of any week. It isn't that I don't have friends. I have a very nice circle of friends, your sisters amongst them, but I...I don't belong with a man like you."

He caught her shoulders and slowly turned her toward him. "Have you ever noticed that women who are called bluestockings are devilishly smart?"

She smiled through what he now recognized was a rather thick veil of pain. "That is part of the definition."

"No, I mean they're intelligent and it threatens those around them. Especially the men who want to believe they have no place understanding history or politics or science or what have you." He leaned in and stroked a finger along the bridge of her nose, and reveled in how her eyes dilated slightly. "But you see, not every man is threatened by a devilishly smart woman. I think you've been hanging around the wrong ones."

"I agree," she whispered, breathless.

"You should keep better company," he continued, even as he lowered his head.

She nodded and tilted her lips to meet his, and once again they were kissing. Just like in the orangery, just like in the billiard room, her lips touching his was like an earthquake through him. Desire struck him with the power he had been trying to convince himself didn't exist and he was helpless to it as she opened her lips beneath his.

He dove in, taking what she offered and reveling in her taste. Like peaches in summer, like wine that would intoxicate him beyond reason. His arms came tighter around her and he molded her against him as his cock began to swell with need.

He wanted her. In all ways, in the most important way. He wanted her and he realized, with stunning clarity, that the longer they stayed on this path, the harder it would become to resist the siren's song of claiming her.

He should have cared about that. Cared about her innocence, cared about the consequences should he steal it, but in that moment, he didn't. He just wanted to give her pleasure and take some of his own.

They sank down together on their knees in the soft grass in front of the lake. He cupped the back of her head and tilted her face for better access as the kiss grew deeper and more heated. She groaned from some deep, primal place and the sound rocked straight to his groin.

He lowered her back in the grass and found his hand moving to cup her breast. She arched at the touch with a gasp of both surprise and pleasure. Her breasts were full and as he stroked one, the nipple grew hard beneath her silky gown. He wanted to see them so badly, to taste them, to strip her bare and prove to her how beautiful she really was.

But that gentlemanly voice inside of him screamed no. Reminded him of consequences before he shut it up again with another deep, passionate kiss.

His hand roamed again, this time to her stomach and then to her thigh. She was squirming beneath him, trying to get closer, breath short against his lips. Finally, he settled his palm between her legs and she groaned low and long.

Even though her skirts and underthings, he felt her heat piercing his palm. He could already imagine it around his cock, squeezing him as he entered her, enveloping him as they became one writhing body seeking nothing but pleasure.

"God, Josie," he whispered.

She murmured some wordless sound of pleasure as she pushed against his hand, seeking out release he was certain she didn't quite understand. How easy would it be to flip up her skirts and give it to her? With his fingers, his tongue, his cock? How easy would it be to steal her innocence and replace it with pleasure? Doing that would bind them forever.

And that one errant thought jolted him out of his passion-induced haze. He looked down at her, eyes glazed by passion, lips trembling, body reaching, and he knew that he couldn't...shouldn't... destroy her future for one moment of passion.

He rolled away from her and sat up with a frown.

"I'm sorry," he murmured as he scrubbed a hand over his face. "I'm so sorry, Josie."

CHAPTER SEVEN

Josie stared up at Evan, not exactly certain what had just happened. He had been kissing her and then he had touched her in those wonderful ways. Her body was on fire, she was trembling with need...

And then he pulled away.

"What?" she whispered.

He got to his feet and paced to the water's edge as she sat up. Realization hit her, humiliating and clear.

"Oh, I see," she said softly. "You don't want me."

He spun around to face her. "You can't really think that. God damn it, Josie, look at me."

He pressed his trousers and she saw the outline of him through the fine fabric. She blushed.

"You might not know what this means, but it means I want you. Very, very much," he said.

She bit her lip and he let out a groan before he turned his back on her again. Panic struck her. He was going to find a way to end this. He was going to walk away even though he claimed he wanted her and she knew she wanted him. And she didn't want to lose this.

She struggled to her feet and moved toward him. "Evan..."

"I'm sorry," he said again.

She shook her head even though he wasn't looking at her to see it. "No, please, let me say something."

He let out a long sigh before he turned back to her. His handsome face was very serious, though she saw his gaze flick over her, drink her in. All hope was not lost. "Yes?"

"I've read books," she blurted out.

His brow wrinkled. "I—what?"

"Well, one book," she corrected. "My father had it in his private study. I was trying to help clean it out after he died and I found the book in this hidden cubby. It had drawings." She shivered as her mind slid back to those drawings. Those very explicit and arousing drawings of men and women engaged in sex acts. "I couldn't read the language, but I could look at the drawings. So I'm not as innocent as you think."

He was still staring at her like he didn't understand and she fought the urge to stomp her foot. She was ruining everything by blathering and not being clear.

"There is a book," she said softly, beginning again. "That I found. And it has pictures of...well, of men and women together." Evan's eyes grew wide and understanding passed over his face and she moved forward with a smile before she continued, "And they show them doing things...well, it's like what you do to me."

"What I do—"

"When you touch me," she explained further.

"Oh," he said. "*Oh*."

She swallowed hard. Now came the more difficult part. "I-I told you before that I knew I wouldn't marry. I accept that. But what I feel when I'm with you, I would like to feel that more."

"Oh," he said again, and turned his face.

She shifted. Had she gone too far? She couldn't tell. Evan was breathing hard and he refused to look at her.

"You don't know what you're saying," he said slowly.

She shook her head. "I told you, I saw a book."

He glared at her. "Josie, a book is not that same as doing the things in the book."

She folded her arms "Please don't treat me like a child."

He laughed, but there was little humor in the sound. "Trust me, I am not. But you're speaking of *ruin*, Josie. And I can't do that. I won't!"

"You can only be ruined if someone else wants you to be untouched," she argued. "And no one does, I assure you. Eight horrible Seasons have proven that beyond need or any other proof. So to me, ruin sounds..." She glanced back at the grass where they'd lain. "Ruin sounds wonderful."

He squeezed his hands into fists at his side. "Josie, please stop."

Her lips parted and she stared at him. Earlier she had said he didn't want her and he had claimed he did. But now she wasn't so sure. After all, she was throwing herself at him, absolving him of guilt, demanding he act on his proclaimed needs and he refused.

So perhaps he was only placating her by pretending. Perhaps once he touched her, he remembered what she was. What *he* was. And that he could have someone so much better.

She blushed. "I'm sorry," she murmured. "I was very stupid."

"No, not stupid," he said, lifting a hand to her before dropping it away like he couldn't, or didn't want, to touch her.

"It is stupid to think you actually do want me. That you aren't just being kind in dismissing me." Tears had begun to fill her eyes and she blinked in the hopes she could escape him without him seeing them. "I can walk home. We aren't far and—"

He moved on her so swiftly that it was as if he was in one moment standing by the lake side and the next he had her crushed to his chest, his eyes bright and on fire.

"Are you mad, Josie? Since you arrived all I have thought about was you. Since I touched you, all I have dreamed about was you. And right now all I want in this world is *you*."

His mouth came down again, this time hard and demanding, and she was forced to give him what he wanted. He drove his tongue into her, proving his desire, stoking her need. She lifted onto her tiptoes and dueled with him, tasting his desire and letting it merge with her own.

She had no idea how long they stood that way, his arms around her, his hands squeezing her closer, his tongue claiming her the way she wished he would in other ways. But when he broke away, she felt bereft.

He stared down at her in his arms and his wild eyes gentled slightly. "Yes, I want you, Josie," he whispered. "But I can't...hurt you."

"But—"

He shook his head. "You say you'll never marry and I see that you believe that to be true. If we went too far, we could be forced to wed."

"I would never force your hand."

He frowned. "Well, even if that were true, the option to marry well could be taken from you permanently. You would be damaged."

"I'm already damaged," she said, thinking of the pitying stares, the ways she was ignored, the sometimes panicked looks when young lords were forced to dance with her. "So I don't care."

"But I do." Evan stroked his thumb over her lower lip with a shuddering sigh.

She shook her head. She could see he had set his mind to this course. She wasn't tempting enough to turn him from it. But her entire body ached in a way it never had before.

"Please," she whispered. "Don't leave me wondering."

She leaned up and kissed him once more, this time soft, this time gentle. She felt him stiffen, then relax into her exploration. And then he pulled away again and it felt like she was being torn to pieces.

"I can...do things..." he said, resting his forehead on hers.

She drew back. "Do things?"

"To satisfy you," he said, his voice rough and deep and seductive. "Without stealing your future."

Her eyes went wide. "How?" she whispered.

He molded her to him as he lowered her back to the grass. "I'll show you."

She settled into the sweet-smelling lawn and watched as he took a long, deep breath. Like he was surrendering. Then he placed his hands on the hem of her skirt and began to push it up.

She tensed as he revealed her legs, turning her face so she didn't have to watch him. She didn't want to see his face if he was disappointed by her body.

He lifted the skirts up and up, pushing them to bunch higher and reveal calf, thigh and finally her hips. He left the dress around her waist and began to touch her thighs, massaging her, parting her legs wider to reveal herself to him.

"God, you are more beautiful than I imagined," he murmured, almost more to himself than to her.

She looked down at him, perched between her legs. Her sex clenched and her heart stuttered. He found her beautiful? She had never considered herself so. Oh, she was no longer the awkward, pudgy girl she'd once been. But she was no lithe wisp either. She had curves, ones that did not exactly fit the fashion of the day. God, how she hated an empire waist.

But here was Evan, touching her, sending fire along her skin, pooling heat and wetness between her legs and he said she was beautiful.

She felt like it for the very first time.

"I'm going to touch you," he whispered.

She nodded. "You're already touching me."

He smiled, wolfish, but also gentle. "No. I'm going to touch you…" He trailed off and tugged at the slit in her drawers, parting the fabric and revealing her sex. "Here."

She stifled a gurgling moan and relaxed back against the grass. She shut her eyes and waited, waited for his hands. Only it wasn't his hands that descended upon her. She felt the steaming heat of his breath at the apex of her thighs instead.

Her eyes flew open and she struggled to her elbows to watch as he placed a hot, wet, open-mouthed kiss against her sex.

What followed that kiss could only be described as a shockwave. Her entire body rippled, her hips lifted and she cried out at the intimacy of the caress and her intense desire for more of the same. He didn't disappoint and dropped his lips to her again. Only this time he stroked his tongue along her length, licking the moisture of her desire away in one sweep.

"Oh God," she moaned.

"Indeed," he growled in return. Then he didn't talk again, for he dove into her like a man ravenous.

He stroked her flesh with his tongue, swirling the rough surface against her tender folders, then spreading them apart with his fingers to reveal more and more. She lifted into him, grinding her hips in time to his strokes as she reached for pleasure.

He gave it to her in powerful measure, sucking at her, tasting her. And finally he dragged his tongue across the pearl of her pleasure, the place she had found herself years ago. She didn't know what it was called, but when she rubbed it, she felt a flutter of sensation like nothing she had experienced before.

With Evan's attention, the pleasure was more than a flutter. It was a torrent, a thunderstorm, an earthquake.

"Please," she panted, dropping her hands to his hair, lifting her hips in desperation. "Please, please."

"You shall be pleased, I assure you," he grunted before he sucked that bundle between his lips. He scraped her gently with his teeth and she cried out. She was so close to something, something she didn't fully understand, but she wanted it so desperately she might have given up breath itself to find it.

Luckily he didn't require that sacrifice. He swirled his tongue around her once, twice, and suddenly her body began to shake out of control. She cried out as electric shocks of pleasure tore through her, starting at the little bundle that he sucked and spreading through every fiber of her being.

She thrashed at the power of her release, her fingers tugging at Evan's hair, her legs shaking, her body weightless as she writhed. It felt like the moments stretched to an eternity, until she was spent and panting, until she could no longer move. Only then did he kiss her one last time, then prop himself to his elbow on his side as he stared up at her.

"Well," she panted as she pushed at her wrinkled skirts to cover herself. "That was something."

He laughed, then helped her bring her skirts back down to her ankles. He rested his hand there, the casual touch nearly as intimate as his earlier ones.

"Well, you said you wanted to experience pleasure. I hope I have obliged."

She nodded. "I've never felt anything like it. Even when I touched myself."

His eyes fluttered shut. "Oh dear God."

"I'm sorry, is that—"

"No," he interrupted, his voice strained. "I'm just trying to be a gentleman and not picture it."

"Oh."

She looked at him while he had his eyes closed. He really was the most handsome man she'd ever known. And he'd done such things to her! But as her gaze flitted lower she realized that his...his member was swollen against his trouser front, rather like the members of the men were in the pictures she'd seen.

"Er, but *you* are not satisfied," she said, pointing without looking as heat filled her cheeks.

He peeked at her. "No, I'm not. Though pleasuring you was quite fulfilling. But you needn't worry, Josie. I have ways of resolving this issue on my own."

"How?" she asked, examining the bulge again from the corner of her eye.

"I will take myself in hand later. And likely think about your taste, the sounds you made when you came."

"Came?"

"Found release," he explained.

"And you will take that...that thing—"

"My cock," he interrupted.

"Oh. Your cock in hand, and what will you do?"

"Stroke it," he said, leaning closer. "Until I find release as you did."

She shivered at the words and was surprised that her body throbbed anew with his description. "I-I would like to see that."

His cleared his throat in what seemed like discomfort. "It is getting late, Josie. We should go back or else your mother will truly worry."

She nodded. "But...but perhaps another time?"

"Do you want to do this again?" he asked.

She bit her lip. "Yes. I want to feel like this if I can."

He seemed to ponder that request for a long moment, then he leaned over her, caging her against the grass with his arms. "So do I," he whispered, dipping his head to kiss her.

She melted into him, tasting an earthy flavor on his lips that she realized was her own. She reached up to thread her fingers through his hair, to draw him deeper, but he pulled away with a shake of his head.

"You shall not seduce me, Miss Westfall. As tempting as you are." He pushed to his feet and offered her a hand to rise. "Now, let us go."

She followed him to the phaeton and let him help her up. She settled into her seat as he joined her and off they went, back toward her home as if nothing had just happened between them. But it had. Every jolt of the carriage reminded her of that. Every side glance at the man beside her.

They rode in companionable silence to her mother's home and he helped her down. He offered her an arm to take her to the door, but she hesitated.

"Evan?" she whispered, uncertain of what to say without sounding foolish.

"Yes?" His dark brown eyes held hers evenly.

"I—thank you for today." She couldn't help the heat that flooded her cheeks and likely made her look like a tomato. "I realize it probably meant very little to you, but it meant a great deal to me."

He stared at her for a long moment. "It meant something to me," he admitted as he released her.

"Did it?"

He nodded. "Goodbye, Josie."

"Goodbye," she said as she stepped into the foyer. But as her mother's butler, Mr. Charles, shut the door behind her, she was not allowed a moment to gather her thoughtsMrs. Westfall flew out of the parlor, hands clasped before her as if in prayer.

"I wondered where you were," her mother gasped.

Josie tilted her head. "I'm sorry, Mama, I didn't mean to worry you."

"Worry me? Posh, you were with a Woodley! How could I worry?" Mrs. Westfall caught her hands and all but dragged her into the parlor. "Now tell me everything that happened! Everything, don't leave out a moment."

Josie gripped the back of a settee to steady herself as images of her afternoon bombarded her. Thoughts of Evan's kisses, *all* of them, melted her insides and made her ache for more.

"There is little to tell," she lied. "We went to visit the tenants as I originally planned and then we took a-a stroll around the lake before we came home."

Mrs. Westfall shook her head. "Oh, no. I think there is more to it."

Josie froze. "You do? What do you mean?"

"He is courting you!" her mother crowed.

"Courting me?" Josie repeated, and tried not to laugh. What Evan had done to her didn't count as courting by any definition. "I don't think so."

"Why else would he take you out today? And keep you out so late?" Mrs. Westfall grinned. "Oh, this will be perfect. You will be married and we will be tied to the Woodley name. A wonderful fit for everyone involved."

Josie pursed her lips. Her mother truly did not understand the relationship she was developing with Evan. Of course, neither did she. She had certainly never guessed he would be so kind to her, nor that he would touch her in such wonderful ways.

It was almost enough for her to hope again. To want something again. Something she had put aside years ago.

And she feared those desires might only lead to heartache.

CHAPTER EIGHT

Evan let out the air in his lungs as he burst through his chamber door and locked it behind him. The room was all but spinning as he moved to the bed, braced himself on the edge and fumbled with the buttons on his trousers. His cock swelled against it, and as he lowered the flap and the warm air hit his sensitive skin, he hissed out a sound of pleasure.

The entire ride home he had been consumed by memories of Josie's kiss, Josie's sweet and innocent desires, Josie's cries of pleasure. And his need had grown with every mile. God, he had nearly turned around, burst into her house and had her right there and then.

But he couldn't.

So he was left with this.

He took himself in hand and stroked over his sensitive skin. Josie had asked about this act, her green eyes wide and bright as she stared at the outline of his erection. What would she do if she saw him do this?

He began to stroke faster, his eyes fluttering shut as he pictured Josie sprawled naked before him, watching him pleasure himself. Better yet, Josie crawling toward him, wickedness in her stare as she took him in hand herself.

He groaned at the images in his mind, coupled with the frantic thumping strokes of his hand.

But Josie touching him wouldn't be enough. He wanted to be inside of her. Some way. Any way. Would she let him press his tip past her lips? Would she swirl her tongue around him like the most experienced bawd? Would she take him all the way to her throat and suck until he could hardly see straight?

He stroked harder at the image, but it still wasn't enough. Because in truth, he didn't want to play games with Josie. He didn't want to tease her and be teased. He wanted to claim her. He wanted to open her legs wide and slide inside her heat, feel her ripple with pleasure around him as she finally understood that book she had described earlier. He wanted to feel her wet heat squeeze him, take him, until he couldn't stand it anymore and he spent.

As that thought exploded in his mind, his body also found release. Hot seed spurted from him and he groaned out Josie's name as he sagged across his bed.

When the world had stopped spinning and he flopped onto his back across the coverlet, he shook his head. When he had first approached Josie, he had been opposed to it. He didn't want to face her hate. Then he had wanted to know what she knew about Claire.

But now everything had changed. He wanted her. And he was drowning in it. He could only hope he wouldn't lose everything before this was all over.

"Where did you go yesterday?" Gabriel asked as he entered the study where Evan had been hiding.

Evan let out a long sigh before he turned to face his brother. "What do you mean?"

"Well, you left the house in the late morning and went straight to your chamber upon your return in the evening. You even skipped breakfast with Mother and me." Gabriel shrugged. "I merely wondered."

Evan gritted his teeth. He had been avoiding his family on purpose but had very much hoped they wouldn't notice his absence quite so keenly since he had very little answer for it. What was he to say? That he spent the day with Josie and had spent the night indulging in erotic fantasies about her?

"I-I was out."

Gabriel had begun moving across the room, but at Evan's tone, he stopped and turned to face him. "Out."

"Yes, that's what I said. Out." Evan folded his arms. "Why? Is that not allowed anymore?"

"And who were you *out* with?"

"I'm the older brother," Evan said, hoping to distract Gabriel. "Aren't I the one who is supposed to interrogate?"

"Not when I have nothing to hide and you do." Gabriel leaned forward. Evan's heart sank. His brother's knack for reading people was about to cause him problems, he could see that. "What is wrong with you?"

Evan sighed again. "I was out with Josie."

"Oh." Gabriel leaned back, surprise clear on his face. "I see. You didn't tell me that was your plan."

"It wasn't," Evan ground out.

"Something happened," Gabriel breathed, rushing to Evan. "What is it? Were you able to extract any information about Claire from her?"

A jolt of guilt hit Evan and he turned away from his brother. Yes, that was what he was supposed to be doing with Josie, finding out about Claire. But he hadn't been doing a very good job at it. Not at all. And now he felt guilt both for trying and for failing.

One way or another, he was betraying someone.

"Look, I came upon Josie about to do a few visits in the shire and I accompanied her," he explained.

"And? Because I know there is an *and* here," Gabriel pushed, this time a bit more gently.

Evan shut his eyes. "There is more to her than I allowed myself to imagine, Gabriel. And when I told you before that I might not be able to see the line between flirtation and something more serious, I was right. Things...progressed between us yesterday."

Gabriel looked at him through narrowed eyes for a moment, but then his meaning seemed to come clear. "Oh. I see. So you...kissed her?"

Evan cleared his throat. "Yes. Several days ago, though. Yesterday I...I went a bit further."

Gabriel staggered back at the admission, his eyes wide and his mouth dropped open. "You seduced Jocelyn Westfall?"

Evan glared at him as he rushed to shut the parlor door. "Say it a bit louder, I'm not sure Mother heard in the garden," he snapped. "God, Gabriel. No! I did not seduce her. Not...not fully, at any rate."

"But you went beyond kissing." Gabriel blinked. "With Josie."

"You keep saying it as if it is insane, but you have seen the girl. She is Venus, she is temptation embodied, she is gorgeous...somehow." Evan clenched his fists. "No one should say otherwise."

"I will admit Josie has greatly improved with age," Gabriel said slowly. "Though she is not exactly my type. But what does this mean?"

"I don't know. She seems to have no expectations or even much desire for a future," Evan murmured, surprised that disappointment clouded his thoughts on that subject.

Gabriel nodded. "Excellent."

"How is it excellent?"

"No, romantic entanglement is always excellent," his brother said with a wave of his hand. "Especially since the reason you pressed her in the first place was Claire. If you wrap her around your finger with seduction, it seems to me that you will be all the closer to either uncovering what she knows through her confession, or through investigation through her things."

Evan stared at Gabriel. "Do you think I feel good about taking advantage of an innocent? Do you think I'm rubbing my hands together in some Machiavellian plan to use her weakness against her?"

"You said yourself she has no assumption that this…this connection between you will lead to a future and certainly you could not want that." Gabriel shrugged. "Why not obtain whatever you can from this opportunity?"

"Do you hear yourself talking?" Evan asked, drawing back from Gabriel in surprise. "You are so obsessed with finding Claire that you are willing to surrender your morals, your values, everything you are?" He shook his head. "Actually, you are willing to sacrifice mine, I suppose?"

Gabriel's jaw set and his dark eyes sparked with emotion. "Claire is our sister—do you not care more about her than some chit who has hated you for over a decade?"

"I care!" Evan burst out in frustration. "Fuck, we *all* care, Gabriel!"

"You say you care, but no one is willing to sacrifice!" Gabriel paced away. "Audrey, Jude, Edward and Mary all went back to London to celebrate their marriages while our sister rots. You're dancing around Josie Westfall like she matters. And all the while Claire suffers."

Evan stared at his brother. He could see the searing pain slashed across Gabriel's face. He could well-imagine it was only intensified by Gabriel's natural tendency to analyze and deduce. He was so tied up in knots by the disappearance of his twin that he was out of control. Almost as lost as Claire was herself.

Evan moved forward and pressed a hand to Gabriel's shoulder. "Listen to me, please," he said softly, hoping to reach his brother through his pain.

Gabriel hesitated a moment, and then nodded. "I'm listening."

"Everyone in our family cares about Claire, Gabriel. Every single one of us would put our lives on the line to bring her home safely if the opportunity arose." Gabriel's face softened a fraction, but Evan continued, "But it is up to Claire to give us the opportunity. It has been made very clear by her actions that she left of her own volition. And even when she realized that Jonathon Aston wasn't who she believed, she has stayed with him also of her own choice. Gabriel, she doesn't *want* to come home."

Gabriel's gaze clouded and he jerked to escape Evan's grasp. "Shut up," he growled.

"I know that is difficult for you. She's your twin, you have a bond unlike any other in the family. But you must accept that it is true."

To his surprise, Gabriel lunged toward him and caught Evan's lapels in both fists and shook him so hard his teeth rattled.

"Shut up!" Gabriel shouted in his face.

For a moment they stood that way, frozen for different reasons. Then Gabriel released him, staggering backward before he fled the room. Evan stared at the open door where his brother had gone, shaken by Gabriel's anger. His drive. It was so intense, so singular of purpose that Evan feared Gabriel might lose control because of it.

"We can't lose another," he murmured.

But what could he do to save Gabriel? Would more information about Claire actually help him? Make his brother come to accept the truth and get out of this loop where saving her was his only drive?

And could Evan's developing relationship with Josie actually do that? Just as Gabriel desired?

"God," Evan muttered as he left the parlor and strode up the hallway. He needed air, he needed space, he needed—

He stopped as he entered the foyer. There, standing next to Vernon, was exactly what he needed more than anything else. Josie.

She was wearing a cream and pink striped gown that fitted her curves perfectly and brought out the brightness of her green eyes. She was utterly beautiful and in that moment, he wanted nothing else but her.

Her gaze slipped to him and whatever she was saying to

the servant stopped as she gaped, her expression telling him she was as moved by him as he was by her. All this inhibitions about her, all his hesitations didn't matter then.

"Miss Westfall," he said as he entered the foyer. "What a surprise."

"G-good morning, my lord," she said, casting a quick glance at Vernon. "I'm sorry to call without sending word first."

Evan waved off the apology and smiled at Vernon. "I can take care of Miss Westfall, Vernon. Please feel free to return to your duties."

The butler gave a quick bow and then scuttled away, leaving the two of them alone in the foyer. Evan stared at her lips. God, how he wanted to claim them. Right here, right now.

Instead, he shook his head. "You are right this is a surprise," he said, desperate to remain appropriate, at least for the moment.

She nodded, though she seemed no less distracted than he was. "Yes," she said, then she shook her head as if clearing her mind. "Yes. I-I came to call on your mother, you see."

He arched a brow at how her voice cracked, at how her hands trembled at her sides. "My mother?" he asked. She gave a jerky nod and he smiled. "You are the worst liar," he whispered as he held out a hand. "Come on, Josie."

She stared at the outstretched offering, and he could all but see her wheels turning in her mind. She was a lady and what he offered her was so not ladylike. But she wanted it. Wanted *him*, and he saw that she was not able to resist even before her trembling fingers intertwined with his.

"Evan?" she whispered, looking up at him in confusion and desire tangled together.

He smiled. "It's all right, Josie. I promise you, I will make everything all right."

Then he guided her out of the house and hoped he could keep that promise.

CHAPTER NINE

Evan hadn't said so much as a word to Josie as they walked down the long path away from the main house. For her part, she could hardly breathe, let alone speak as he guided her away from safety and toward the unknown. A metaphor if she had ever experienced one. And yet, she didn't feel unsafe with him. She felt...right.

Which likely made her an idiot of the highest order, but it didn't matter. She wanted this. Wanted him. The moment he touched her, she knew she wouldn't resist in the slightest.

"Where are we going?" she asked, thinking of the way Evan had pleasured her by the lakeside the previous day. Her body still tingled with the memories.

He smiled and motioned toward a little cottage at the bottom of the hill. "There."

She drew back. "The caretaker cottage?"

He nodded. "Jude Samson lives there when he accompanies my brother to this estate, but I doubt he would argue with my borrowing it while he is away on his wedding trip with Audrey." He stopped and opened the door. "Not that I would ask his permission in this moment."

He allowed her through and she entered the little cottage. It was snug and cozy, even romantic with its rustic furniture and the small space. Through an open door she saw a room with a big bed, and she shivered.

How far would she go? How far would he?

"Why wouldn't you ask his permission?" she asked, her voice shaking as he closed the door behind them and put them in utter, complete and highly inappropriate privacy.

"Because if he said no, I wouldn't be able to do this." He moved on her, cupping her face gently, tilting her into the proper position and dropping his mouth to hers.

She heard the hungry sound of desire that seemed to come from her very core as she lifted on her tiptoes and met his heated kisses.

"My God, I have thought of nothing but this," he whispered as he broke their kiss and rested his forehead against hers.

"Nor have I. You must think so little of me for being a wanton."

He pulled back. "Because you came here?"

She nodded. "I hoped I would see you, Evan. I hoped this would happen."

He laughed. "Then why would I judge you? The moment I saw you standing with Vernon, my heart soared. And trust me, after the morning I've had, I needed that. Needed you. Need you now."

"Then please don't deny yourself or me," she whispered.

He met her gaze, and she recognized the fire of his expression. He was going to give her such pleasure. And she hoped that this time, with the privacy of this place, she would be able to do a bit of the same for him.

He took both her hands and guided her back through the main room of the cottage and into the bedroom.

"I want to see you," he whispered as he began to unfasten her dress. "May I?"

She blushed. "You may be disappointed."

He frowned. "Impossible."

She said nothing else as he slowly unbuttoned and unhooked her. When he slid his warm hands beneath the silky fabric of her dress, she hissed out pleasure, but the pleasure faded as he shoved the gown off her shoulders and left it in a heap at her feet.

She was only in her chemise now. And there was no hiding herself in just that thin scrap that clung in all the wrong places. He stared. He stared so long that she found herself lifting her hands.

"I'm sorry," she whispered.

He jerked his gaze from her body to her face. "What in the world are you apologizing for?"

She fought for words, but they were too painful, so she opened her arms and motioned to herself. "This."

"This beautiful body that is made for me to worship it? No apologies necessary," he whispered as he reached out to trace a finger along her collarbone.

She shivered at the touch. "I am not the way women are meant to be. I know it. The fashions of the day are for slender women. My body is not slender. I have curves and...and..."

"And you think this makes you not the way women are meant to be?" he asked, moving closer. Close enough that she could feel his heat.

She nodded, keeping her gaze away from his. The last thing she wanted to see was his agreement with her statement. Or worse, his disgust. But she felt his finger slide beneath her chin and he lifted her face.

"Right now I want you to listen to me. Don't hear the voices of those who teased you, don't hear your own voice that batters you, just listen to me," he said softly. "When I look at you, I see perfection. Your curves are what make you lovely. You are soft and beautiful, warm and welcoming. And I want to do such wicked things to that gorgeous body."

She stared at him. He looked so very sincere and his heated words curled into her body and soul, wrapping around the ugliness of the past and shielding her from it, if only for this moment. This moment she wanted to last forever.

"Show me," she whispered, her voice trembling.

He nodded as he pushed his hands under her chemise straps and stripped the last bit of fabric away. She shivered as the cool air in the still room hit her, shivered as his eyes moved over her. She was naked. In front of a man. In front of *this* man.

She examined his face for a flash of disgust, disappointment, but there was none there. His dark eyes only dilated with desire as he reached out to cup her naked breast.

She sucked in air at the shock of his touch. His fingers were so warm against her and her body clenched of its own accord as he let the pad of his thumb circle one distended nipple.

"Perfect," he breathed, and heat flooded her cheeks at that simple declaration.

"I—" she began, then stopped herself.

His gaze eased up from her naked flesh to meet her eyes. "You?" he pressed. "Don't hold back, Josie. If you want something, say it."

She swallowed hard. "I want to see you."

His eyebrows lifted at that request. "Naked?"

She nodded swiftly. "Yes."

The corner of his mouth turned up, creating that blasted dimple in his cheek. The one she currently wanted to trace with her tongue.

"It's a fair bargain," he said, backing away from her to shrug out of his jacket.

She licked her lips as he tossed it aside and went to work on the knot of his cravat. He parted the top of his shirt and she clenched her fists at her sides. The triangle of smooth skin, a little too tan for a proper gentleman, made her ache between her legs. An ache that grew as he tugged buttons open and pulled the shirt free from his waistband. He pulled it away and tossed it aside tossed and she heard a little sound escape her lips.

"Was that a peep, Miss Westfall?" he teased as he opened her arms to let her see.

She nodded. "Very much a peep," she admitted. "I just...I've imagined...and pictures...oh, and statues...but never…never this."

He smiled at her stammered, broken words and moved closer. "Would you like to touch as well as look?"

"Yes," came her strangled reply. She reached out her hand, watched it tremble before she laid a flat palm on the broad plane of his muscular chest.

His eyes fluttered shut and a curse escaped his lips as she let her palm glide down, over hard muscle, over warm skin. Urges washed over her. She wanted to flatten her breasts against him and rub like a cat, she wanted to trace all the ridges and valleys of his body with her tongue.

She wanted to do anything to get closer to him. Anything.

Her fingers reached his waistband and she glanced up at him. His eyes were still squeezed shut, his breath short as she stroked him. But she wanted more. With a shiver, she began to open the buttons that closed the flap of his trousers.

His eyes flew open and he stared down at her. "What are you doing?"

She smiled. "Trying to see the rest, my lord."

"Well, who am I to stop you?" he chuckled, tilting his hips to allow her better access. It took a moment, but she finally freed him and dropped the flap. When she did, she gasped out loud.

There it was, his member.

"Statues make this look much, much smaller," she murmured.

Now his chuckle became a full laugh. He tilted his head back, exposing the corded tendons of his tanned throat, and his laughter filled the room, lessening her fear, making her smile even in this moment so charged with emotion and desire and anxiety.

He made it all so…*easy.*

"Yes, I fear the sculptors of the world really didn't do us a service, did they?" he asked. "But I am real, not made of stone."

"Are you sure?" she asked, staring at his member once

more. It did seem very large. And it was hard, curling against his belly in a dominant display.

"Touch me and see," he whispered, all the humor gone from his voice and his eyes.

She blinked as she stared at him, stared at *it*. "How?" she asked.

He smiled as he reached out to catch her hand. He lifted it to him and closed her fingers around his length. She jolted at he feel. Velvet over steel, warmth and strength combined.

"Oh," she gasped, smoothing her fingers against him as she explored him.

"Yes," he moaned, his tone broken. "*Oh*."

"I'm not hurting you?" she asked, watching his face twist.

He shook his head. "On the contrary, your hands feel like heaven."

"Yesterday, you said that you would stroke yourself to find relief," she said, blushing once more at how frank her words were. She cupped him and began to slide over him gently. "Did you do so?"

"Jesus," he breathed, his head dipping back over his shoulders and his breath shortening.

"Did you?" she repeated as she stroked a little faster.

"Did I?" he asked. Then he shook his head. "Oh, yes. Yes, I did. Last night."

She shuddered at the thought of him doing what she was doing. "What did you think about?"

"About tasting you," he grunted. "And about claiming you."

Her knees shook. Claiming her. Taking her innocence. "That's what I thought about last night too," she admitted softly.

She stroked a few more times and he let out a heavy cry. Then his seed spurted from his body, covering her hand. She used the slickness to stroke a few more times before she released him. She stepped back, blinking at him.

"Was that right?" she asked.

He nodded. "God, yes."

He bent and drew a handkerchief from his jacket pocked, then reached out to draw her close. Gently, he cleaned his essence from her fingers. She stared up at his face as he did it, marking every flutter of his lids, every movement of his lips.

He looked down at her upturned face with a smile, then lowered his lips to claim hers. She opened to him without hesitation, loving the slide of his tongue, the taste of his desire merging with her own. He let the handkerchief flutter away and wrapped both arms around her.

Now they were naked skin to naked skin, hardly an inch separating them, and she arched to get closer. He was so warm around her, she felt protected and cherished. And even stronger than those feelings was the need. A heartbeat of need in her veins, between her legs, transformed into the song of her soul.

"You are unexpected," he said as he broke the kiss and moved her toward the bed. He lowered her to the coverlet and settled himself over her.

"In a bad way?" she asked, using a finger to smooth an errant lock of hair away from his forehead.

"Not at all. In fact, in such a good way that I think you deserve a reward."

He leaned down and his mouth covered hers again. She sighed into him as she wrapped her arms around his neck and reveled in the wicked sensation of skin on skin. There was nothing better, really.

Nothing better until he slowly stroked his hand down her side, making her shiver and shake with pleasure. He shifted to move beside he and she groaned with the loss of his weight pressing her into the bed.

"Trust me," he whispered. "It will be worth it."

She blinked up at him, lost in his stare. He held her there, his captive, and returned his hands to their roaming. He dragged his fingertips to her breast and began to stroke them back and forth across the sensitive skin. She arched with a hiss of breath and he smiled.

"You are very responsive," he murmured. "How responsive remains to be seen."

He pressed his mouth to her neck and began to suck there, plucking her nipples in time to his kisses. Josie was lost. She knew it and she didn't care. Nothing in the world mattered in that moment except the sensations rushing through her body.

At the lake the previous day, she had felt such pleasure, but what was building in her now felt even more powerful because her entire body was involved. Evan was seducing her from the roots of her hair to the tips of her toes and she couldn't help but arch beneath his hands and moan into the quiet.

He eased downward, kissing her shoulder, her collarbone, and finally his lips met his fingers. He sucked her nipple into the hot cavern of his mouth and sucked hard. Hard enough that her heels dug into the bed.

She opened her legs without hesitation, clenching against nothing as he lapped at her sensitive flesh. And then she felt his fingers at her core. She had been so distracted by his mouth she hadn't even realized he had moved his hand. But there it was, his fingers gliding her folds open, stroking over her gently.

"In that book you talked about yesterday," he murmured against her skin, pressing kisses between her breasts in a trail to the one he had left neglected. "Were there any drawings of a man touching a woman like this?"

Josie struggled for breath. He wanted her to remember details? She could scarcely recall her name.

"Yes," she panted.

"A man with his fingers inside a woman?" he pressed even as he gently probed one fingertip inside her.

She gasped at the intrusion. "Yes, yes!"

"Mimicking a man's cock taking her," he continued.

She nodded. She was beginning to understand her wicked readings all the more now.

"This is what I would do with my cock," he explained. "If I could have you."

He pushed inside, gently stretching her. She gaped down at his cock, thinking about how it had looked hard. A finger was one thing, but *that* inside of her? It seemed impossible.

"And it would feel good," he promised. "After the pain." She looked at him, wide eyed, and he shook his head. "No pain today, sweet. I won't break your hymen, so all there will be today is pleasure."

She nodded, trusting him despite their past. Despite her doubts.

He started to stroke his fingers, and she forgot everything else. It was magic what he did, finding some hidden place inside her that bloomed beneath his attention, throbbing in time to his touch. And she realized, with a start, that what he was doing was very much like what she had done to him with her hand just a short time earlier. He was thrusting into her body just as she had thrust over his.

And it was divine. He returned his mouth to her nipples and the world went blurry as she focused only on the pleasure building between her legs, the electric pull of his lips and teeth. She was so close to that final release—*coming*, he had called it. She began to shake, her fingers digging at the bedclothes, her head turning to the side as she reached, hoped...

And then he pressed his thumb against her clitoris and the world blossomed with color and beauty. Her inner muscles spasmed and pleasure flowed through her, rocking her to her very center.

She cried out, clinging to the bed, clinging to him, knowing he was watching her through the crisis and not caring about the show she put on. All that mattered was this exquisite pleasure and the man who had brought it to her.

She collapsed back against the pillows as the tremors faded, reaching for him, drawing him down to her lips. And knowing that this stolen moment in time was worth anything that had come before and everything that might happen afterward.

CHAPTER TEN

Josie smiled as Evan climbed back into the bed with her and tugged a knitted blanket around them. She curled into his side, his arms folding around her. Together they stared into the fire he had just built for their comfort.

"Have I mentioned how pleased I am you came to visit this afternoon?" he said with a grin that softened his features and her heart.

She laughed. "I'm not sure if you did, but I gleaned your pleasure from the way you moaned."

"Miss Westfall!" he gasped, feigning shock.

"Have I gone too far?" she continued to tease.

He shrugged. "Perhaps there is no such thing in this circumstance."

She frowned rather than smiled at their banter. In her mind, there wasn't such a thing as too far. She wanted everything physically possible between them. But Evan wouldn't give her what she desired. He insisted on protecting her innocence despite her thoughts on that subject. But he had made himself clear, hadn't he? He would not change his mind.

Or would he?

She glanced up at him again, intent on opening the subject a second time, but what she saw on his face stopped her. Evan was still smiling, but she noticed something as the firelight flickered over his taut jawline and full lips, and reflected in his dark brown eyes. There was sadness in his stare.

All thoughts of her own desires fled as she saw that unexpected expression. She had known Evan for more than half her life and she had never such a look on his face. He always made himself appear wholly confident, relaxed, jovial, at ease, always the perfect, popular gentleman. But seeing these deeper emotions, the ones that she sometimes felt in her own heart, touched her.

She leaned up and touched his cheek, smoothing her palm over the rough evidence of his facial hair returning despite the close shave he normally wore. He looked down at her, their gazes locked and that pain she had noticed seemed to magnify. His eyes went wide and he attempted to turn his face, as if he could escape what she saw, but she held him gently, not allowing him to avoid this connection.

"What is troubling you?" she whispered.

He stiffened further and shook his head. His cheek scraped against her palm and it took everything in her not to sigh at the touch.

"Troubling me? Nothing at all, I assure you, Josie. Nothing except how much I want to kiss you again."

He leaned in and there was such temptation to give in to his distracting techniques. She knew where his kiss would lead and she'd told herself that was all she wanted from this man.

But there was a desperation in his voice that brought her up short. And so she dodged his lips with much reluctance.

"Evan, I can see you."

"Of course you can," he retorted, wrinkling his brow.

"I mean, I can *see* you," she said again. "Not just the mask you wear of how jovial you are that you show the world. I see *you*. And I can see something is troubling you. After everything we've shared, can't you tell me what that is?"

He tilted her chin up, and for a moment she thought he might continue to use the sexual heat between them against her as a wall to keep her away from anything deeper. But instead, he simply stared into her face.

"And just when did you develop the ability to see me?" he

asked, his tone low and, she thought, a little shaky.

She shrugged. "Maybe once you kissed me? Maybe once you touched me? Or maybe it's just that when you are broken, you begin to recognize the signs of it in someone else."

His lips parted. "I am not broken."

She tilted her head. For the first time she saw that his words were truly a lie. Even with his charmed life, Evan wasn't whole. Just as she sometimes didn't feel whole.

She had never felt so connected to him as she did in that moment, even when he touched her.

She stroked his cheek again, smoothing his skin. He leaned into her palm, almost as if he couldn't stop himself.

"Not broken, then," she said softly, trying to maneuver around his resistance. "Bruised, though."

His jaw set and she saw him battling with his desire to keep her out of his emotions and his desire to seek comfort in a friend. In the end, he merely nodded once. "Perhaps a bit bruised," he admitted.

Her heart soared at those words, not because his pain gave her pleasure, but because he was willing to admit even a small piece of it to her. She knew how hard that had to be to him, this man who always seemed so perfect. Now she saw that was by design, a mode of operation meant to keep others at arm's length.

And this was him cracking the door for her to know him better.

"Earlier you said something to me about needing me after this morning," she pressed, delving delicately into the dangers of his heart. "What did that mean? What happened this morning?"

He cleared his throat gently and she saw him struggle once again.

"You know you can trust me, don't you?" she pressed.

His gaze jerked to her face and flitted over her. She held her breath as he looked, seeking and searching. Then he nodded. "Yes. I suppose I know I can," he said, but there was not much pleasure in those words. She thought she heard guilt in his tone. Likely over the cruelty that had resulted from his words in the past.

But right now that was the furthest thing from her mind. She took his hand and lifted it to her chest. "How can I help you?"

He turned his face forward to look at the fire again and was silent for a long moment. Then he whispered, "It's Gabriel."

She blinked. She wasn't certain what she had expected when she asked the question, but his response was not it. She shook her head. "Gabriel?"

He nodded. "We had—" He cut himself off and she could still see what a struggle it was for him to talk about this to her. But he finally caught a breath. "We had a bit of a row this morning."

"Over what?"

"He wants me to do something I do not feel right about. And he believes if I don't then it proves I don't care about Claire."

Josie stiffened at the mention of her friend's name. She shouldn't have been surprised, of course. The loss of Claire had been the catalyst for a great amount of turmoil and pain for the Woodley clan.

"I know Gabriel is troubled, as you all are," she said softly.

"Of course we are all troubled, but I fear Gabriel takes her loss the hardest."

She watched his pained expression, the way his jaw set as he spoke of his lost sister, and she shook her head. "I'm not sure about that."

"What do you mean?" Evan asked, leaning forward, as if desperate for any tidbit about his sister.

She chose her words carefully. "Gabriel is her twin and of course they have a strong bond, but you shouldn't discount your own bond with her, or Edward's or Audrey's or your mother's. You are all hurting, Gabriel does not own the only share of loss."

Evan seemed to consider that for a long moment. "I do feel her loss," he admitted. "And I wonder if I could have done anything to help her. Was I so selfish and blind that I didn't do anything to save her when the option was right in front of me?"

Josie froze. She had made promises to Claire to keep her secrets, but now her will was being tested. Here was Evan, his eyes filled with pain, his hands clenched on the bedclothes, and he needed her to console him.

"I am certain you couldn't have changed your sister's path," she said, hoping that would be nonspecific enough a statement.

But Evan's hawkish stare lifted to her face immediately, and she saw his focus. "She talked to you before she left, didn't she?"

"She did."

He shook his head. "But you can't know her heart now. Just as I can't. The only person she makes any contact with is Gabriel. And she shares little, even with him."

Josie held her breath, considering her options for a moment. She wanted to help Evan. But she didn't want to be used.

"Evan?" she began.

He locked eyes with her. "Yes?"

"You—you aren't only doing this because of Claire, are you?"

He blinked. "Doing what?"

She swallowed hard past the lump of anxiety in her throat. "You aren't using me, using this connection between us, as a way to get to Claire, are you?"

His face went unreadable in a second. She tensed, uncertain if he had shut down because she was right or wrong.

"No, Josie," he finally said softly. "I'm not using you."

She let out her breath as relief washed over her. This was real. It was just *them*. Nothing else.

She nodded. Knowing that, she could be more honest. "You say Claire only writes to Gabriel, but that isn't true."

Evan tilted his head. "It isn't?"

She fought to find a way to say the words, a way that would keep her promises and yet ease his pain. "I—Claire has been writing to me as well."

He pressed his lips together, and she felt his body tense beside her. "Josie, you don't have to—"

"But I will. At least as much as I can. Claire has written to me a handful of times since she left."

His eyes went wide at her admission, but then he leaned in. "What does she say?"

Now she balked. Some of the things her friend had said would be hurtful. And she didn't want to be the one to break Claire's confidence or her lover's heart.

"I'm certain our letters are not so different from the ones she writes to Gabriel."

"But your eyes do not say certainty," he pressed, leaning closer.

She bit her lip. She'd meant to comfort Evan, but it seemed she had failed.

"I can say no more," she whispered. "I only mentioned it in hopes it would give you some relief to know that she reaches out to more than one person. That I *know* you couldn't have done things differently because your sister has told me so."

"But there is more to it than that," he insisted. "What did you say to me earlier? I can *see* you, Josie."

She held perfectly still for what felt like an eternity as she struggled for a response to Evan's pressure, his pain. "Then perhaps you can see that I am not able to tell Claire's secrets any further. Please don't ask me to."

"How can I not?" He frowned. "My sister writes to you and apparently gives you details about her life. Do you not love her enough to share them with me? In case I could help her?"

Her jaw set at his suddenly accusatory tone. "Don't you *ever* question my love for your sister, Evan!" she burst out, surprised by the sudden strength in her voice and in her heart. "Ever."

He drew back and a bit of the wildness left his eyes. "I'm sorry. I'm sorry. I know you love her."

"And because of that I can't betray her any more than I have already done," she said, pushing the covers aside and searching around on the floor for her discarded clothing. He watched but made no attempt to stop her, and that stung.

"Then I must ask you a similar question to the one you earlier posed to me." His eyes narrowed. "Is this reluctance to reveal more a way to get some twisted revenge for how I treated you as a girl?"

Josie had been tugging her chemise over her head, but she spun around to face him at that quiet question. "How dare you? You truly think I am so petty as to keep facts from you out of revenge? Is that how low you think of me?"

"No," he said, getting out the bed. She blinked at the sight of him, still naked, his skin highlighted by the fire.

"Claire has her troubles," she said, trying to focus on the matters at hand and not how beautiful his body was. To combat those thoughts, she tugged on her dress and began to button it. "But she *doesn't* want to be found."

His face twisted in anger, growing red as he stared at her. "And you get to decide that?" he snapped.

"No," she retorted, her voice elevating. "She does."

His mouth opened as if he had something else to say, but then he shut it abruptly. There was a part of her that was pleased she could frustrate him even a little.

And another part that wanted him to understand her position, not hate her for it.

"Listen to me, Evan, and try to understand what I'm saying to you. Since Claire left your family, she has had so much forced on her, taken from her. She will come back when she is ready to do so."

He stared at her, his pain plain on his face. It twisted her gut to see it there.

"You don't understand," he whispered.

She turned her head. Here she had felt a connection to him, a true sense of belonging. And yet she was still an outsider to him, even after all they had shared.

"Don't I?" she whispered. "I lost her too. And unlike you, she was all I had."

She didn't wait for his retort—she simply turned her back and left the cottage. Left him. But she couldn't leave the searing pain that hit her belly, not only because she was reminded of all she'd lost in Claire.

But because it was clear that she had likely lost the tenuous relationship she'd begun to build with Evan too.

CHAPTER ELEVEN

"Why did Mama insist we attend this ridiculous party?" Gabriel asked as he approached Evan and handed over a watered down drink.

"I have no bloody idea." Evan shot a glance toward his younger brother. It had been two days since their unpleasant encounter in the parlor. Two days since he had last touched or seen Josie.

For Gabriel's part, he seemed intent on ignoring the ugliness that had flared between them. Perhaps that was just as well. At this point, Evan was reluctant to discuss anything of real merit with Gabriel. Pretending their row hadn't happened was likely best for all involved.

With Josie it was more complicated. He had spent the last forty-eight hours running over every moment of their last conversation together, analyzing what had been said and done between them.

And he was stuck. On one side was the guilt he felt. Josie had flat out asked him if he was using her desire for him against her. And he had lied. He had done *exactly* what Gabriel wanted and leveraged their physical connection in order to obtain information about Claire.

On the other side was an equally troubling realization. He could see now that the desire, the need, the connection he was building with Josie was about more than just his lost sister. He missed Josie's touch. He missed the easy passion between them that seemed to come from nowhere and yet had become so damned important to him. And it had only been two days.

"Do you think she's hoping we find wives?"

Evan shook his head at his brother's question. In truth, he had all but forgotten Gabriel's existence at his side, anyone's existence at that moment, when he was obsessing over Josie. He blinked.

"What? Who?" he asked, trying to focus.

His brother tilted his head. "Mama. Do you think she's so pleased by the recent matches of Edward and Audrey that she is hoping by sending us to this soiree we will come home with ladies to court?"

Evan pursed his lips. Honestly, he wouldn't put such a plan past their mother, especially now that she was recovering so nicely from her fever. She was bored sitting in her bed all day. Likely she *was* plotting.

"If that is her desire, she will be sorely disappointed," he said. "There is certainly no one here to tempt—" He cut himself off as Josie stepped into the room with her mother. "Me," he finished, the heat gone from his declaration.

She was utterly lovely in every way. From the way her dark hair was twisted and curled so that little tendrils of it framed her heart-shaped face to the way her full lips pressed together as she searched the room. She wore a light green dress with elaborate gold leafing stitched into the skirt, all of which brought out the brightness of her eyes and the porcelain perfection of her skin.

His mouth went dry. Her gown clung perfectly to her curves, those curves he knew so damned well. And his errant mind took him to images of getting her alone and stripping away every layer of fabric to touch and pleasure what lay beneath.

"Oh look, it's Josie," his brother said before he took a sip of wine. "How are things going with—"

Before Gabriel could finish his question, Evan walked away, moving across the floor toward her. He watched as her mother wandered off to speak to a friend, watched as Josie maneuvered her way to the edge of the room to find a place along the wall where she could disappear. A pang of guilt twisted his gut as he thought of why she felt that way.

He kept an eye on her as he moved through the crowd, dodging her gaze so he could observe her unseen for a moment. He was standing behind a pillar near her when he saw two young women whispering. He leaned in to hear.

"...wallflower," one of the young ladies was finishing before she glanced toward Josie.

He glanced at her and saw Josie could hear the women as clearly as he could. She lifted her chin and stared off into the crowd without saying a word.

"Well, I don't know why she even comes anymore," another of the young women said with a catty giggle. "Who would want her?"

"You'd have to ask *Horsey* that," the first girl said with a toss of her head that was likely meant to see if Josie could hear them. "I wouldn't know."

The window of vision before Evan's eyes suddenly went red at the words he heard. He clenched his teeth, tightened his fists and stepped out from around the pillar. When he came into view, he heard Josie gasp and watched as the two young women who had been gossiping about her straightened up to smile at him.

"Oh, I didn't see you there," said the first. "Good evening, my lord."

Evan ignored her sudden politeness as he looked from one to the other. "Lady Veronica, yes?" he asked, pointing to the first girl, a brunette who he might have once called rather pretty, though she was anything but to him now.

She blushed. "Oh goodness, sir, I had no idea you knew who I was."

"The Earl of Littleton's daughter," he continued. She nodded enthusiastically, but before she could speak Evan turned his attention to her companion, a curly haired blonde with blue eyes she batted at him relentlessly. "And you—you are the daughter of Sir Trestworth."

"I am," the young lady supplied with a slight incline of her head. "Charmed to make your acquaintance, I'm sure."

He shook his head. "You think I am *charmed* by you? Charmed by your rudeness and childishness?"

He looked over to find Josie staring at him, eyes wide and hands clasped in front of her.

"I—well—but—" Lady Veronica stammered.

"I heard how rudely you addressed Miss Westfall," he continued, motioning to Josie.

The young women turned, and at least the brunette had the wherewithal to gasp as if she were surprised. "Oh goodness, Miss Westfall, I-I didn't see you there."

Josie shook her head. "Didn't you?" she said quietly.

"I think you did," Evan continued. "And you were nasty, vile little creatures. And it is funny, you know, because I think the true reason you are such nasty, vile creatures is because you look at Miss Westfall and you are *jealous*."

"Jealous?" Lady Veronica and Josie repeated together. Lady Veronica just sounded confused, but Josie's tone was incredulous.

He turned his attention back to Josie. "Jealous because when Miss Westfall walked into the room, the attention of half the men went to her. How could it not?"

Josie held his gaze for a few seconds, then turned away with a frown. He forced himself to look at her tormenters again. What he was about to do, to say, would perhaps not reflect well on him. But in that moment he did not care. The world didn't matter. Josie did.

"I want you to understand something, and I want you to pass this information along to all your catty, simple little friends. The something is this: no one will ever call Josie by the name 'Horsey' again, is that clear? If I hear of that nickname being used, I will find out who did it and I shall make sure they are made to be very uncomfortable socially.

Now go back to your guardians and try to hold yourselves with a little more grace in the future."

The young women gaped at him, but Lady Veronica recovered herself first. She turned to Josie and muttered an apology, then grasped her friend's arm and dragged her away. Once they were gone, Evan moved toward Josie. He expected her to turn her gaze toward him with gratitude. At least he hoped she would be pleased. But instead when she looked at him, her cheeks were filled with high color and her bottom lip trembled.

"Excuse me, my lord," she muttered, and then pushed past him to exit the room.

He stared at her retreating back, utterly confused by why she had reacted so strongly to his defense of her. And all he could do was follow to find out why she was not thanking him for his aid.

Josie flung herself into the first open parlor and slammed the door behind her. She paced along the length of the room to the window and stood there, staring out at the dark garden as she tried to calm her rapidly spiraling thoughts.

And of course behind her, the door opened. She didn't have to turn to know who had followed her. And yet she did, and found herself face to face with Evan.

He was devastatingly handsome in his fitted evening clothes. More devastating was the confused and hesitant look on his face as he closed the parlor door and leaned against it. They were alone. Inappropriately alone. For a moment, her upset over what he had done faded and she wished she could go to him. Touch him. Forget everything in his arms.

"Josie," he said softly, and the spell was broken.

She took a long step in his direction.

"Why did you do that?" she hissed, wishing her voice

didn't crack and reveal her hurt, her embarrassment, so clearly.

He drew back. "Do what? Defend you?"

She shook her head. "Oh God, Evan, that was the least of some of the taunts I've had to endure over the years."

He flinched and she saw his regrets mirrored in his eyes. "You never should have been treated that way."

That simple sentence hit her straight in the gut, but she ignored how much the words meant. "Don't you understand? The best course of action is to ignore them when they start. To not show them that they cut you to the bone. To not reveal your underbelly and give them another place to stab."

He blinked. "You think my words made you more vulnerable?"

She shrugged, reliving that moment when he had stepped out from his hiding spot and confronted her tormentors. Hadn't she thrilled for a moment that a knight had come to rescue her at last? Hadn't it been magnificent to watch the color drain from those ugly faces? Or hear them stammer apologies?

But then there were the other things she'd seen. Like those around them leaning in, whispering. Like the eyes that had followed her from the ballroom.

Evan had made her the new center of attention. And that was one place she had no interest in being. It was too bright there, too dangerous. All her flaws would be amplified.

"Oh God," she whispered, turning so she didn't have to look at him. "Of course I'm more vulnerable."

"I don't understand why," he insisted.

She looked at him again and smiled at his naivety. "Oh Evan. Lovely, popular, handsome Evan. You have always been the center of attention, haven't you? You are a flame and all the moths gather and dance around you. You can see no danger in that because you are charmed and beautiful."

"Don't speak like I'm a child," he grunted, folding his arms.

"But in this you are," she continued. "You've probably never felt the sting of cruelty. You've never wanted to just disappear into the ground and never come back. You've never prayed that you'd wake up invisible."

"What does that have to do with what I just did?" he asked softly.

She tilted her head. "They were all watching, Evan. Listening. When I walked into the ballroom tonight, I was an unimportant girl who had once been chubby and had a nickname used to tease her. As soon as you decided to become my champion, all the curiosity in the room became focused on me. Right now they are talking about me. And I assure you that much of the talk isn't good."

"How can you know that?" Evan said with a shake of his head. "That they are talking about you and that it is not good?"

"Because I've stood on the wall watching them do it to me and to others for years," she said, throwing up her hands in frustration. "I felt them staring at me as you spoke, I felt them watching me as I left the room. I'm sure they watched you as you followed me. And right now they are whispering about what exactly I must have done to inspire Lord Evan Hartwell, handsome second son of the House of Woodley, to defend me. They are reminding themselves that I was ugly as a girl, they are trying to decide if I am still ugly—"

"Enough," Evan said, holding up a hand. His teeth were clenched and he drew a few breaths. "If they are talking about you, Josie, I assure you that it isn't to talk about how ugly you are."

"Why wouldn't—"

"You have told me what I don't understand, now it is my turn to school you." He moved closer. "Josie, when you walked into the ballroom, the eyes were already following you. Mine, yes, but I saw other men tracking your movements. I watched their eyes light up with interest, lust. I hate it, but it's true."

She shook her head. "That is not possible." She blinked several times but he never looked less than utterly serious. "That cannot be true."

"But it is," he said softly as he reached out a hand to trace the curve of her cheek. "You are beautiful, Josie, desirable."

"I have curves that aren't fashionable," she said, though it was hard to think when his fingers were stroking her skin like that.

"When it comes to men, curves are always fashionable," he whispered. "In truth, that is likely the cause behind any teasing that still goes on. When women see men look at you that way, they would be fools not to be jealous."

"Jealous of me?" Josie snorted, but the words touched her. "That is a laugh."

"Laugh all you want." He leaned closer and his breath whispered over her lips. "It's true."

His mouth brushed hers, light and gentle, and it took everything in her not to melt against him, surrender to him. Instead, she stepped back.

"If they all want me so much, then why do I have no suitors?" she asked.

"When was the last time you were asked to dance?" he asked.

She shrugged. "I don't know. In London. Some god-awful gathering at Almack's, I suppose."

"Did you say yes?"

She frowned. "He was the brother of one of my tormentors. I declined."

"I see. When was the last time you actually said yes to a man who approached you?" he pressed.

She shifted. "I...I don't rightly remember."

He smiled as he reached out to tap her lightly on the tip of her nose. "That may be your answer, Jocelyn Westfall. You have made yourself very mysterious, which men find alluring, I assure you. But you have also made yourself unreachable."

Was that true? She had turned down partners because she had doubted their motives. She had doubted herself. Was Evan right that in doing so, she had cut herself off from true connection?

"I...I built my own wall?" she whispered.

"Perhaps. Though you were the prettiest flower along it, I assure you."

She felt like she couldn't breathe. "What you say makes no sense to me."

He nodded. "I know. Because you let what others say about you as a girl sink into your skin. You began to doubt yourself, to believe them. And eventually it was your own voice that berated you."

She dipped her head. "That—that might be true, yes."

"You can stop that voice any time, Josie."

She stared at him. Here he was, so utterly handsome, and he could not possibly understand. "It isn't so easy as that."

He stepped closer once more and her heart all but stopped as he reached out to take her hand. He lifted it to his chest and held it there so she could feel the steady throb of his heart.

"If your voice refuses to be kind, then replace it with mine." He squeezed her fingers gently. "Jocelyn Westfall is beautiful. And desirable. And kind. And so very arousing. Jocelyn Westfall, you deserve better."

She blinked and all thoughts of her childhood troubles or her current embarrassments faded. In that moment all she could see or think about was the man before her. The complicated, frustrating, wonderful man who held her hand and confused the hell out of her.

"What are we doing?" she whispered.

His eyes went wide at the question, and for a moment he didn't speak. She saw him struggling, trying to find the answer she herself didn't know or understand. Finally he shook his head. "I'm not quite certain, Josie? Are you?"

"No," she admitted as she allowed him to draw her closer. "But I like it."

His eyes went wide and his smile broadened. "Even though you hate me?" he teased gently.

She refused to tease back, not when he was so close. Not when everything in her world was tightening in concentric circles to just him. Only him. Always him.

"A lady doesn't hate," she murmured.

He laughed, but his focus never wavered from her face. "Strongly despise me?"

She reached up to cup the back of his head and gently drew him to her. Just before she touched her lips to his, she whispered, "Not anymore."

CHAPTER TWELVE

Josie leaned up into Evan's lips, drinking him in like he was water and she had roamed the desert for days. Being apart from him seemed like forever. Being with him now felt like the only thing that mattered.

He was stiff for a moment, almost surprised by her kiss, but then his arms came around her and he molded her closer, tilting his head so he could angle their kiss deeper. She opened to him and explored him in return, tasting every inch of him with all the passion she had ever felt.

All the love she was beginning to feel.

But no, she would not think about that. Not right now. Right now all she wanted was to feel Evan's arms tighten, to feel his passion rise, to give in to pleasure and desire and everything that boiled between them.

She arched against him and he let out a low moan that broke their kiss.

"You are killing me," he muttered.

"It's only a little death," she whispered back.

He leaned away. "And how do you know about *le petit mort*?"

"I read books. I told you. And you've taught me plenty about it, haven't you?"

He made a low growl deep in his throat—it was a possessive, masculine sound, and her body clenched as moisture began to pool between her thighs.

His mouth covered hers again and she drove her tongue against his, tasting him, feeling him, drowning in him. He pushed her backward across the room until her legs touched the settee. She trusted him as he lowered her against it and covered her body with the solid weight of his own.

She cupped the back of his head, holding him steady as he made love to her mouth and set her body on fire with longing. She arched beneath him, rubbing her body on his, and he moaned with pleasure and pain mixed.

"Josie, we can't," he murmured even as he dragged his lips down her neck. "Not here."

"Please don't deny me," she whispered, grasping her own skirts and tugging them up between them. "Not when I need you so very, very much."

He shook his head, but she could see he was lost. She had power over him, at least when it came to this. He had needs, and right at this moment, she wanted to use them.

She wanted more than he had ever given before. She wanted it all.

His hands slipped under her rapidly rising skirts and he found her sex. He stroked one finger across the wet slit and shuddered out a sigh.

"Damn it," he growled beneath his breath.

She smiled at his frustration. "Sit up," she whispered. "Perhaps we can pleasure each other together."

He stared down into her eyes, seeking out something there for so long that she feared he might see into her very soul. Then he did as she asked. He tugged her to a seated position and placed himself next to her. With a flick of his wrist, he unfastened his trousers and popped free, already hard and heavy.

She couldn't help herself. She reached for him, taking him in hand and stroking him from head to base once, twice. His eyes squeezed shut and he rested his head back on the settee with a moan.

"Josie," he whispered, her voice a warning, a prayer, a

caress.

She continued to smooth her hand over him, studying his face as he lifted into her, watching as desire and pleasure rolled over him. As she worked, he stole his own hand back between her legs and began to gently stroke her.

She sighed with pleasure, but deep within her there was something else. Frustration. Oh, she knew they could bring each other to completion this way, sitting next to each other, their hands free to explore. But she didn't want that. She wanted more. She wanted everything.

She wanted it now.

She thought of that book she had stolen all those years ago, thought of the pictures it showed. Of women straddling their men, taking them inside for that final act of passion that Evan denied her.

She jolted against his questing fingers and cast a side glance at him. His eyes were still closed, he was focused on the pleasures they each gave. In a moment, she could straddle him, open to him. He had denied her that final act before, but what would he say if she was right there, her wet heat teasing him, demanding what she wanted?

He might be angry later, but she wanted this. She wanted to know pleasure and possession now in case she never had this chance again.

She held her breath as she swiftly moved, straddling him in one fluid motion. His eyes flew open as she positioned her sex against his cock.

"Josie!" he gasped, his pupils dilated with excitement and pleasure mixed with horror.

"Please," she whispered, arching over him, feeling the tip of his cock nudge her and aching for more. "Please let me."

"You can't," he murmured, but she ignored him and began to slide over him. "My God," he growled as he grasped her hips. "You are like heaven."

She met his gaze and held it there. "Please, Evan. Please don't stop me. Please don't turn me away."

His lips parted and she could see his struggle. Animal versus gentleman. Future versus present. Need versus reason. And in the end, he let out a shuddering sigh. The grip on her hips tightened and he began to gently ease her down over him. There was a burst of pain almost immediately as he slipped inside, and he held steady.

"There," he said, his voice low and gentle. "Now you have been claimed."

She swallowed as the pain began to fade and she was aware of his width in her, stretching her, making them one body. The thought aroused her further and she looked down at him.

"That is all?"

"No," he said with a grim smile. "Not even close."

He lifted up slowly and more of him entered her, more and more until she felt their bodies fully meet. Her eyes went wide as she stared down at him.

"It is very full," she whispered, flexing her hips a little to test the feeling. A shot of pleasure met her at the act, and she gasped.

"Oh God, that is what you need to do," he moaned. "Move just like that. Over and over, Josie. Move like that until you come."

His rough voice, the desperation in his tone, spurred her on, and she did exactly as she had been told. By instinct, she rolled her hips over his, finding the places where the movement gave her pleasure, observing how it affected him. He watched her as she did it, his eyes wide and filled with lust. That look drove her, the feel of him inside of her drove her and she thrust over him in a ceaseless rhythm that lifted her higher and higher.

So high that she could almost taste release. She could feel it coming, and then it was there. With a soft cry, she was overcome by the bursting dam of pleasure, the rippling spasms of her body.

He groaned and in a smooth motion, he caught her by her

backside and flipped her over on her back on the settee. He was still inside of her, and as her pleasure rolled over her he began to grind his hips against her, thrusting relentlessly, lifting her orgasm to even more intense plains.

And just when she thought she could take no more, just when her vision began to blur and the world tipped precariously out of control, he let out a groan and she felt the wet heat of him fill her.

He collapsed against her, holding her tight to him, his body still molded within her. She curled against him, spreading her fingers against his chest to feel his heart pound in time to her own.

It was done. She was no longer a virgin. She had experienced passion at its fullest extent and oh, how she had loved every moment of it. Loved every moment with Evan. Now, even when this was over, she would still have this memory to cling to on nights when she was sad to be a spinster.

Evan shifted, and suddenly he pulled away from her. Their bodies parted and she shivered at the loss of his warmth. She watched as he stood, tucking himself back in place, buttoning his trousers, removing all evidence that they had done something so beautiful.

Finally, he looked at her. Glanced at her, really, for he would not hold his stare on her for too long, and her heart sank.

"Josie," he began.

She pushed to her own feet, smoothing her gown over herself. "Oh, please, Evan. Please don't say this was a mistake."

"But it was," he whispered, turning his face from hers. "What I have done."

"You've done nothing." She reached for his arm. "Look at me."

He did so, but slowly, like he didn't want to face her. "You know what you say isn't true. As a gentleman, I should not have allowed this."

"I asked you to have me," she insisted. "I knew what I

wanted and you gave it to me."

His lips pursed and he pulled his arm from her grip and paced away. She watched him move restlessly about the chamber, watched his unhappy face whenever he turned and allowed her to see it.

"Evan, I do not expect anything from you," she whispered. "This was not a trick, not a trap. I wanted to feel passion and you gave me that gift. Now I know what it is like to be desired and claimed and I can live with whatever the future brings. Think of this as a gift you've given me. I thank you and I absolve you of any guilt you may feel over what just transpired."

He stopped pacing and looked at her. Really looked at her, and she felt like he was almost seeing her for the first time. She shifted under that hard, focused stare.

"Josie, I claimed your innocence. And I spent inside you, so we might have created a child." He shook his head. "Propriety—nay, *honor*—dictates what must happen next."

Josie could hardly breathe as she watched him begin to move toward her. "Evan—"

"Josie, we must marry."

"Honor," Josie repeated, and Evan flinched at the suddenly flat and emotionless tone of her voice. Just a moment before it had been filled with excitement, pleasure and the remnants of desire.

Oh, he had gone too far. Worse, he had *known* how out of control he was allowing the situation to become, perhaps from the first moment he had touched Josie. But when she had pressed her sex to him, when he had felt her humid heat and saw her trembling need, reason had been crushed. Honor had been silenced.

He could not have denied her in that moment any more

than he could deny himself breath. Taking her had been everything he'd dreamed of and more.

But now there were consequences.

"Honor, Evan?" she repeated again.

He nodded. "Yes. Josie, what I've done is unforgiveable. What we've done could cause a lifetime of consequences for us and for our families. The only thing we can do, whether we want to or not, is to marry."

Her face twisted, her cheeks filled with red heat, and she backed away. "Why, you are a romantic, my lord."

He frowned. "You want romance in this moment?"

She shook her head. "No, Evan, I don't want anything in this moment. I got what I wanted already. But I never asked for more." She moved even further away, closer to the door. "And while I thank you for your kind offer to lower yourself to be my husband, I am afraid I have to decline. Good evening."

He stepped toward her to stop her, but she had already turned the handle and yanked the door open. But before she could escape, she came to a sudden stop, for right in the hallway was Gabriel.

"Ah," his brother said with a slight smile for Josie. "There you two are. You've been missed."

Josie shifted and shot Evan a quick look over her shoulder. Her hurt was plain on her face. But so was her strength. Strength he wanted to lean into, to share.

"Well, then I should get back," she said. "And it is lucky you are here, for I'm certain your brother has a great deal to discuss with you. Good night, gentlemen."

She shoved past Gabriel and hurried away, leaving Evan in his place like he had been glued there. Gabriel leaned into the hall to watch Josie go and shook his head.

"What did she mean by that?" he muttered, then came into the room and shut the door. "Or, wait, did she tell you something about Claire?"

Evan fisted his hands at his sides and paced away from his brother. "Not everything is about Claire, Gabriel."

"No, of course not," Gabriel muttered. "So you don't know anything new."

"I know a great deal of new things," Evan mused, thinking of the way Josie's tight body felt pulsing around him in pleasure, the way her face looked when he filled her. "Just not about Claire."

Gabriel shook his head. "What is going on?"

Evan scrubbed a hand over his face before he looked at his brother again. Gabriel was too observant for Evan to pretend nothing had just happened. And in truth, he needed to talk about this with someone he could trust. There was no one in the world he trusted more than his brothers.

"Josie and I..." he began. "Josie and I made love."

Gabriel stared at him, blinking and unspeaking, for what felt like an eternity. "Made love? As in made love, made love? As in sex?"

Evan glared at him. "That is what making love means."

Gabriel took a long step back. "I-I—"

"Well, I have shut you up," Evan drawled. "I suppose that is a point in my favor, at least."

"I'm sorry, I'm just...shocked." Gabriel moved across the room and sat down, happily in a chair before the fire and not the settee where Gabriel and Josie had just been so entangled.

"Why are you shocked? It isn't as if this hasn't happened before," Evan said softly. "Men take women every day."

Gabriel shook his head. "You and Edward were never libertines, but I know you both had your dalliances here and there. Still, there is a difference between you tupping an obliging widow or the occasional light skirt and taking Josie, who is...*was* an innocent!"

Evan heard the judgment in his brother's tone and it rubbed raw along his own guilt. "I thought you wanted me to do anything necessary to obtain any information Josie had regarding Claire."

Gabriel flinched. "I did say that. And I suppose now that you are...you are *physically* connected, there will be increased opportunity to press for that information. But, Evan, I never thought you would go so far in seduction! To *take* her like this? This is our sister's best friend. This is a lady. This is...this is wrong."

Evan stepped away, not able to look at his brother and see such horror on his face. Gabriel was only voicing every thought in his own head. He was just as torn as his younger brother, only over slightly different reasons. While Gabriel was caught between the wrongness of the act and the potential for gain, all Evan could think about was how he had stolen something precious from Josie. But how he wanted so desperately to do it again. And again. And again. Until she was his in every sense of the word.

Gabriel wouldn't understand that. Hell, Evan hardly did.

"What are you going to do?" Gabriel asked.

Evan let out a long sigh. "Well, there is only one thing a man can do in such a situation, isn't there? Even if the lady resists."

Gabriel drew back. "You don't mean..."

"Yes. I intend to marry her." He thought of Josie's hurt, her refusal, just a short time ago. "One way or another, Jocelyn Westfall will be my bride."

CHAPTER THIRTEEN

Josie sat at her mirror, staring at her face in the reflection. She didn't look different. It seemed like she should after such a life-altering event as last night. But she didn't.

With a sigh, she stood and paced away from her reflection and all the things she didn't want to see.

"How can you be so confused when you actually got everything you ever wanted?" she asked the open window and the breeze that took her words away into the world.

Except what she said wasn't exactly true, was it? She had managed to convince Evan to take her at last, but afterward everything between them had been so complicated. So charged and changed. Evan had looked at her, but it was no longer the same. Now she was a burden he had to carry, a point of honor he had to see through even though he didn't want to do so.

How she hated that.

There was a light knock on her door and she turned with a false smile. "Yes?"

When the door opened, it was her mother standing there. Josie braced herself for whatever was to come. "Good morning, Mama."

"Good morning," her mother replied cautiously. "You do not look like you slept well."

Josie frowned. "Of course I did," she lied.

Mrs. Westfall let out a sigh. "Do you want to talk to me about something, Jocelyn?"

Josie's lips pursed. If her mother was calling her by her given name, she must be concerned, indeed.

"What do you think I have to talk about?" she asked, hoping her tone sounded light instead of shrill.

"At the ball last night—"

Josie turned away. "I'd rather not discuss it."

Mrs. Westfall stepped closer. "Yes, so you have said ever since the moment we left, and I gave you your space, but now I must demand that you talk to me."

Josie shook her head and looked at her mother again in confusion. "Why?"

Mrs. Westfall let out a long, heavy breath. "I know you think of me as the enemy because I push you toward a future that frightens you. But you must know I do it out of love."

At her mother's sad tone and hurt expression, Josie leapt forward. "No, Mama, I don't see you as the enemy at all."

Mrs. Westfall frowned. "I wasn't ever an outcast, nor were your sisters."

Josie pinched her lips together, some of her desire to sooth hurt feelings fading. "Yes, I know. I am a disappointment. We have had this discussion so many times."

"No, that isn't what I meant," Mrs. Westfall said with a shake of her head. "What I meant to say was that I didn't know what to do when you were teased. And until last night when Evan defended you in front of the assembled throng, I don't think I fully realized how deeply you were hurt and how completely you were sometimes isolated." She moved forward and took her hand. "I should have come to your rescue, I think, as he did. And I'm sorry."

Josie bent her head. There had been times she wished someone would ride in like a hero and protect her. And hearing this heartfelt apology meant so much to her.

"Mama, it wouldn't have changed anything," she said softly. "Claire defended me many times and the worst of the tormenters continued on, just not in her presence. It would have been the same with you. As for Evan…"

She trailed off, for she had no idea what to say on the subject of him, especially to her mother. What they shared was not at all appropriate.

"He seems to care for you," Mrs. Westfall said slowly, almost carefully, like she feared the response.

Josie flitted her gaze to her mother and found her looking expectant. "You can stop looking like a cat who has finally cornered an elusive mouse. There is...there is nothing between us. I will still likely die a disappointing spinster."

"That is the second time you have claimed I am disappointed in you," her mother said, moving closer and cupping her cheeks. "And I am not. Josie, you are unique. You are lovely. You are kind. Do I want you to find happiness with a husband and home and family of your own? Of course, but because I think you would be content in that life. But I could *never* be disappointed in you."

Josie blinked at the sudden tears in her eyes. "You couldn't?"

"No, of course not!"

"Then why push me so hard in the marriage mart?" Josie asked.

Mrs. Westfall wiped a tear from her cheek. "Because I feared if you weren't pushed a little, you wouldn't even give another option a chance."

Josie considered that. Her mother was right, of course. If she had been left to her own devices, she likely never would have come out at all. She would have stayed in her room with her books and only gone out when Claire dragged her away.

"Now may we briefly return to the subject of Evan?" Mrs. Westfall said softly.

Josie paced away. "There is nothing to say on that subject," she said through clenched teeth.

"People were talking when he defended you, when you two disappeared together for so long, Josie," her mother said. "And now I must ask you, you say there is nothing between you, but is that true? Is there something going on that I should know about?"

Josie caught her breath. She could dance around the truth. That was something she had taught herself to do quite well over the years. But right now her mother was asking her a pointblank question. And lying outright was not as easy.

She turned slowly and found her mother standing by, waiting, her arms folded and a look on her face that did not allow for lies.

Josie worried her lower lip, trying to find words, explanations, some way out of this conversation.

"I—" she began.

But before she had to finish that sentence, there was another knock at her door and then her maid, Nell, popped her head into the room.

"Oh, I'm sorry to interrupt," the young woman said with a deferent nod to Mrs. Westfall. "But you have a visitor, Miss Jocelyn."

Josie wrinkled her brow. "A visitor?" she repeated.

Nell nodded. "Yes, miss. Lord Evan Hartwell is here."

Josie took a long step back, as if putting space between herself and her maid would make the truth disappear. "I—tell him no, tell him—"

Mrs. Westfall frowned. "Nell, you will tell the gentleman nothing. We will be down in a moment."

"Yes, ma'am," Nell said with an odd look for Josie before she left the room and Josie and her mother were alone again.

"Mama," Josie began.

But her mother held up a hand. "Jocelyn Westfall, between your refusal or inability to answer a simple question about Evan and this desire to avoid him, it is clear something is between you two. You *will* go and see him."

Josie could hardly catch her breath. She shook her head. "Please don't make me."

"Oh, darling. Hiding from whatever it is you feel or whatever it is you've done will do no good. Trust me. Your heart will follow you wherever you go. So you might as well put your chin up and face that young man. *Now.*"

Josie had a strange and powerful urge to revert back to childhood. To throw herself onto the rug, dig her heels in and refuse. But that had never worked as a girl, and from her mother's stern expression now, she could see it wouldn't work any better.

She was going to have to face Evan. And she had no idea what to do or say once she saw him.

Evan paced the parlor where he had been sent to wait for Josie. How long had he been waiting? It seemed like an eternity. Would she not see him? Was that how far she was willing to take this refusal to be his bride?

God, he would have to push past servants and barge into her chamber. In the worst case scenario, he might even have to admit to her mother that he had seduced her. Together they would force Josie to see reason.

Only, as he paced across the room one more time, it wasn't reason that made his mind spin. No, it was something else. Honor might have brought him here, but when he pictured Josie as his bride, it went beyond that. To have her by his side forever? To be able to do what they'd done at the ball the night before, but do it slowly? Over and over?

That sounded like pure perfection.

The door behind him opened and he spun to face the intruders. He tried not to frown as Mrs. Westfall entered the room. She smiled at him, then looked over her shoulder at the empty doorway.

"Oh, great God," she muttered. She stepped into the hallway and dragged Josie into the room. She gave her daughter a look of exasperation as she shoved her forward, then smiled at him again. "Good morning, my lord," she said. "What a wonderful surprise to have you call on us. Isn't it,

Josie?"

Evan arched a brow. Josie did not look wonderfully surprised. She looked pale, drawn and perhaps a little nauseated. He almost wanted to laugh at the way she glared daggers into him, like he had ruined some plan of hers.

But when he thought of how her plan was to avoid a future together, he couldn't laugh. There was nothing funny about the fact she would run away.

He couldn't let her do it. He looked at her mother and realized he had an ally in Mrs. Westfall.

"I'm very happy to be here," he said, choosing to address only Josie's mother.

"Please sit," Mrs. Westfall said, motioning to a chair as she all but dragged Josie forward. "Would you like some refreshment?"

"No," he said, shooting a side glance at Josie. She was glaring back. He smiled at her. "I am fine, thank you kindly. I think it would be best to simply get down to the reason for my coming here straight away."

Mrs. Westfall sat on the settee, pulling her daughter down beside her. Josie folded her arms. Of course, that only served to push her breasts up just a fraction and whet his appetite for them all the more. How could she have ever thought her curves to be a mark against her? He adored them.

"And what is that?" her mother asked brightly, drawing his attention away.

"I have come here, Mrs. Westfall, in order to ask a very important question."

Josie sat up straight and jerked her gaze to her mother, then back to him. She leaned forward, her eyes wide and her cheeks pale. He saw her fears and her panic there, but also a tiny flicker of something else. Right there, plain as anything, was the connection between them that had only grown in the past few weeks.

That connection that made this far more than just an act of honor.

"Oh, please don't," she whispered.

He met her stare evenly. "Josie, it's all right."

"Please don't do this," she repeated.

He frowned at her desperation. He had created that in her. And he hoped to take it away soon enough. But for now he had to focus on matters at hand. He smiled at Mrs. Westfall, who was staring between them as if they were crazy.

"I have come to ask for your daughter's hand in marriage, Mrs. Westfall," he said. "I would like to take Josie as my bride."

CHAPTER FOURTEEN

The world felt like it was spinning and Josie couldn't make it stop. She stared at Evan, watched him mouth those words. *I would like to take Josie as my bride.* It was a dream. It was a nightmare. It was both.

Mrs. Westfall leapt up and the spell was broken. Reality crashed in as her mother clapped her hands together.

"Oh my!" she gasped.

Evan rose too, leaving Josie the only one who couldn't find the strength in her legs to move. She could only watch them, an observer in her life. But then, she always had been, hadn't she? Allowing others to dictate how she behaved or felt.

"Yes," Evan said, but he was watching her.

"This is so unexpected," Mrs. Westfall breathed. "I knew you and Josie were spending a great deal of time together since our arrival, but I did not guess you were becoming so close that marriage was becoming a possibility. I just—"

Mrs. Westfall looked down at Josie as she spoke and suddenly her words trailed off. She stared at Josie, saw her collapsed back on the settee, and a shadow crossed her face.

Mrs. Westfall straightened up a bit and turned her attention back to Evan. "You know, my lord, I realize my daughter has said nothing in regards to your proposal. And in the end, it is her choice."

Josie slowly stood up, shocked that her mother would say such a thing and not simply rush her into the wedding Mrs.

Westfall had always dreamed of for her.

"Mama?" she whispered.

Her mother reached out and took her hand, squeezing gently. "If you have come here, Lord Evan, to obtain my permission to ask for my daughter's hand, of course I grant you that. You come from a good family, a family that has been a friend to ours for years. I know you to be an honorable and decent person."

At those words, Evan shifted and Josie saw his guilt. The guilt that reminded her why he was doing this in the first place. Her heart sank.

"But my permission and my daughter's are very different," Mrs. Westfall continued. "So I will leave you now so that you two may discuss this in private."

Josie's lips parted and as Mrs. Westfall moved toward the door, she followed.

"What are you doing?" she whispered.

Her mother smiled at her. "No more pushing, Josie, I promise you," she said as she touched her daughter's cheek. "But perhaps you could make me a promise as well."

"What is that?" Josie asked, her voice trembling just as her hands were. Just as her heart seemed to be.

"No more running, either." Then Mrs. Westfall smiled and left the room, shutting the door behind her.

Josie stood, her back to Evan, staring at that shut door for what seemed like an eternity. It must have seemed the same to him, for finally he cleared his throat.

"Josie, won't you look at me?"

She fisted her hands at her sides. When his voice was so gentle, it made her forget why she was refusing his proposal. But she had to remember. She had to.

She turned and hoped there was steel in her expression as she folded her arms. "You should not have done that in front of my mother."

"It was a dirty trick, I know," he admitted. "I would say I was sorry, but the fact is that when I saw your face, I realized we were at war. And I needed an ally. What I did was an act of desperation."

She pursed her lips. "We are not at war, Evan," she said softly, but the words seemed hollow. Hadn't they always been at war, in a way? As children, as lovers, and now.

"It didn't work at any rate," he said. "She took your side. But then, I suppose I should have expected it. Your mother loves you."

Josie shifted. "Yes. She does. I saw that in a whole new way this morning."

He nodded, though he couldn't understand. It was just Evan believing his charmed life was everyone's. He had no idea how her world had been all but set upon its head by her mother's sudden acceptance of Josie's decisions.

"Josie," Evan said softly, and he took a long step toward her. He was still five feet away, but it was already too close. She didn't want to feel his heat or smell his skin or be seduced by his touch.

Well, she did want all those things. But she couldn't give into him now when he was demanding something so permanent.

"Don't," she whispered.

"You keep saying that, but you can't run from this now," Evan replied, his tone still dangerously gentle and kind. "We must face this. We *must* marry."

Her stomach dropped. "*Must* marry," she repeated. "There goes your honor again, Evan, dragging you into things you don't want." She heard how hard her tone was but wished it was even stonier. "And my answer is the same as it was when you offered to 'save' me last night. I won't marry you. Not like this. I wanted what happened between us in that parlor and I will not change it or be forced into misery with you because you have some desire to flagellate yourself over it."

She paced to the window, but behind her she heard Evan sigh heavily. She wanted to face him. God, she wanted to *comfort* him. But she wouldn't. She couldn't.

"Last night I didn't do this the right way," he said slowly. "And I seem to be making a muck of this today as well. So let me try again. Josie, this proposal is not about self-flagellation. It isn't about honor."

She spun on him with a snort of derision and he smiled ever so slightly.

"It isn't *only* about honor—is that more correct?"

She blinked. "I don't know. *Isn't* it only about honor? That you want to save me from what we did? That you want to prove to yourself that you aren't some bastard who claims virgins and then leaves them?"

"I don't come off well in that description," he muttered.

In that moment, that charged, desperate moment, she actually wanted to laugh at his quip. Instead she shook her head. "God, you are so self-assured. You think if you are funny or charming, I'll fall over myself to be yours. Well, you can't tease your way out of this."

"And you can't run your way out," he retorted swiftly.

He moved on her again, and now the distance between them was only three feet. Three short strides and she could be in his arms. She could simply accept what he offered and ignore that he didn't *want* to offer it. She could pretend her way into this marriage.

But would she be happy? Could she be if she looked into his eyes every day and saw...*resignation*?

"I won't be your trap," Josie said.

He met her stare and his expression softened. "You won't be," he said. He cleared his throat. "I have always been better at sarcasm than truth, I fear. A mechanism to protect myself, Audrey and Claire would say. So it is not natural to me to speak what is in my heart. But I'm going to try and I hope you will forgive me if it isn't perfect."

Josie froze. What was he talking about? What was he doing?

"Jocelyn Westfall, from the moment you returned to the shire and I saw you at my sister's wedding, I have been...captivated." He frowned. "You must understand I did not want to be captivated. You were Claire's friend as a child and you made me feel guilty about being an ass toward you when we were young. But nevertheless, I couldn't stop thinking about you."

Josie shook her head. "I—"

"Please, let me finish." When she shut her mouth, he continued, "The first time I kissed you in the orangery, I knew I was lost. I wanted to kiss you all the time, I wanted to do more than just kiss you. It was very confusing since we hadn't exactly gotten along. And considering the fact that you are a lady and my entire life I have been told not to feel such things for ladies, or at least not to act on those feelings."

"But you did," she whispered. "We did."

He nodded, and there was a hint of a smile in the corner of his mouth. "Oh yes, we most certainly did. And it was wonderful, Josie. But never enough. Nothing was ever enough with you. I touched you, I wanted that touch to be more intimate. I held you, I wanted to hold you even longer. And that was wrong. But I did it anyway."

She swallowed hard. His words were so sweet, so gentle, so romantic that she could hardly breathe or think or respond. Yet she knew she must.

"But—but why did you do it?" she asked, needing to hear that answer. Needing to know what had driven him as much as she needed breath or light or peace.

He locked eyes with her, the dark brown holding her hostage without even a flicker of hesitation. "Because I wanted you. And here is the part that may make you hate me."

She caught her breath. Hate him? "What part?"

He cleared his throat. "I could have said no to you last night when you wanted to make love in the parlor. I could have pleasured you in some other way. Or set you aside and ended this affair as I should have many times. But I didn't, Josie. Now, part of that was because the passion between us addled my mind. My body wanted what it wanted and that powerful need overrode reason. But another part was also there. I took you because in some way I wanted it to come to this."

"This?" she asked.

"This moment where I am standing before you, asking you to marry me, Josie."

He moved forward again at last and Josie almost sagged with relief as he reached for her hand. When he took it, warmth spread between them, up her arm, over her body. It was the heat of her desire, yes, but it was also the warm comfort of home. Of everything she had ever wanted and feared she'd never have.

It was, she realized in a flash, the undeniable embrace of love. She loved him.

With a gasp, she looked up into his face. His handsome, angular face. She loved everything about it, from the soulful depths of his brown eyes to the dimple that popped in his cheek whenever he laughed. She loved him.

Which was as terrifying as it was wonderful. And yet she wasn't afraid. She was calm and accepting of that feeling. As if it had always been a part of her, even if she hadn't fully recognized it.

She swallowed because she knew he was awaiting some kind of response. Slowly, she recalled how to form words and said, "You think you wanted to trap yourself?"

He shook his head. "Not trap. Please stop saying trap, for it implies I'm unhappy to be here. What I'm saying is that somewhere deep inside of me, I wanted this, Josie. I made it happen through my actions. And I'm *not* sorry."

He lifted her hand to his mouth and pressed a warm kiss to her knuckles. She shivered at the gentleness of the caress, the way he held her gaze while he did it.

"Evan—" she whispered.

"I care for you, Josie," he interrupted.

She hesitated. Cared for her. Not loved her as she did him, but perhaps that would be foolishly asking for too much. Caring for her was very good, more than she had ever hoped to ask for.

"You do?"

He nodded. "Indeed, I do. So I am asking you again if you would be my wife."

Every word that had come out of his mouth had been said with such passion, such honesty. But she still hesitated. Because she wasn't sure. Because the future he offered her was so wonderful and terrifying at once.

He tugged her a little closer so that she was pressed against his chest. She could feel his heartbeat and it was fast, like he was nervous.

"You know it is the right thing to do," he said, his voice low and rough. "And not because of honor, but because we both want to do a lot more of what we did last night. Because we both know it could be a happy life."

She swallowed. How could she deny him when everything he said was just putting words to her greatest hopes?

"But—but I hate you," she whispered.

He smiled. "Do you now?"

"Yes."

He leaned in and pressed his forehead to hers. "Yes you hate me or yes you'll marry me?"

Now it was her turn to smile even though she was shaking. "To both," she said.

He said nothing, he declared no more. He simply dipped his head and kissed her. She lifted into the kiss, wrapping her arms around his neck, opening for him as he tasted her, surrendering herself and her future to his care. For now. And for always.

CHAPTER FIFTEEN

"And so we are engaged!" Evan felt Josie's hand tighten on his bicep as the words left his mouth.

For a moment, the gathered group of his family, her mother and Miss Gray all stared at him, then her, then him again. Josie continued to smile, but he saw the paleness of her skin increase, the light in her eyes begin to fade.

But then the surprise passed and his mother rose from her seat slowly. "How wonderful!" she burst out as she crossed the room and embraced Josie. "But what a surprise!"

The entire room became a hubbub of happy activity, with felicitations exchanged and everyone talking at once. Over the throng, he heard Josie's mother admit, "I fear I knew. After all, we did ride over here together."

The mothers began to laugh and their heads immediately went together, likely chatting about the wedding plans soon to come. Evan's attention went to Gabriel. He watched as his brother approached Josie and said something softly to her. She smiled, but the nervousness was still in her gaze. Then Gabriel moved to him. Their eyes locked, but Gabriel said nothing, only shook his hand slowly.

Perhaps his brother would have talked to him then, would have brought up the concerns that were bright in his eyes, but before he could, Evan's attention was brought elsewhere. Quietly, Josie slipped from the parlor through the terrace door.

His stomach sank. Being the center of attention had never

been a good thing for his future bride. It was clearly hard for her to accept it even now.

He moved to intercept her, to follow her, but before he got three steps away from his brother, there was a soft hand on his forearm. He glanced down to find Mrs. Westfall standing at his side.

"We didn't have time to speak privately once you and Josie gave me your news and we flitted straight here," she said. "Your mother and brother are now talking and it seems Josie has gone outside, so perhaps we could take a moment?"

Evan glanced again toward the terrace. He knew Josie was outside, and he guessed she was not out there because she was happy or comfortable, but he didn't know how to refuse her mother's request without seeming rude.

"Of course," he said, motioning toward the other side of the parlor where they would have a bit of privacy. "Come."

She followed where he led and smiled up at him. "I have always liked you, my lord."

"Evan," he said. "Just Evan now that we are to be family."

Her smile faltered a little. "That is what I must ask you about. Your relationship with my daughter has come on very, er, quickly."

He pursed his lips. "Yes," he agreed slowly.

"She has not always had a very easy time," her mother said, a shadow crossing her face. "Perhaps I should have done more, helped her, intervened when she was being mistreated."

"We both have our regrets on that score," he said softly.

Mrs. Westfall's eyes went wide. "Do you?"

He nodded. "I may have inadvertently contributed to Josie's pain," he explained. "And though she has forgiven me, I find it harder to forgive myself."

"Is that why you stood up for her at the ball last night?"

Evan stiffened. The ball last night seemed a hundred years away now, as did his defense of Josie against the cruelty of those around her. "Yes."

"I am glad she has found a champion. But I admit I still

have concerns."

"Concerns?" he repeated. He was truly surprised about that. He would have thought Josie's mother would be over the moon at her daughter's engagement. After all, she had been pushing Josie to find a husband for years.

He found himself suddenly happy Mrs. Westfall's earlier attempts had met with failure.

"It is hard, I think, for Josie to trust those around her." Mrs. Westfall shook her head. "With good reason."

"Yes." Evan frowned as he thought of his ulterior motives when he first pursued Josie. What would she think if she knew his initial reason for approach was information regarding Claire, even though he had claimed otherwise?

"I'm sorry, I'm being silly, I'm sure. I only mean to say that I hope you will take care of my daughter. That you will be mindful of her emotions."

"I will, Mrs. Westfall. I assure you I will do all I can to take the best care of her."

His future mother-in-law looked at him, stared at him, and he felt her sizing him up. He wasn't certain of what she decided upon, though, for she hid her reactions well. In the end, she just smiled.

"Good."

Quickly she changed the subject and began chatting with him about wedding plans. But even as she spoke, his mind wandered to Josie on the terrace and if he would truly be able to keep his promise to protect her. From the world. And from himself.

Josie leaned on the top of the terrace wall with her forearms, staring out at the garden below. The warm breeze stirred her hair, the birds chirped happily around her, and yet she felt very disconnected from all she saw.

Her thoughts were just so tangled.

Back inside, everyone was talking about her wedding to Evan. But she had felt every second of their hesitation after the announcement of their betrothal. Perhaps none of them could believe a girl like her could catch a man like him. Perhaps even though they liked her well enough, they were trying to hide their shock, their feelings that she didn't deserve him.

And if his family felt that way, she could only imagine the whisperings around London when word reached there.

"I'm sorry to disturb you…"

Josie turned at the feminine voice from behind her. The person who had intruded upon her reverie was Lady Woodley's healer, Miss Gray. As the other woman shut the parlor door behind her, she smiled.

Josie returned the expression. The young lady was truly lovely, with dark red hair that was bound up properly, though the curls were undeniable and a few bounced around her face. She was pale and porcelain and slender, almost the exact opposite of Josie. Exactly what men liked in a woman.

And once again she wondered if Evan had ever noticed his mother's healer, even though he had earlier claimed he hadn't.

"Hello, Miss Gray," Josie said. "You didn't interrupt, I was just…just…"

"Getting some air?" the other woman offered helpfully.

Josie nodded. "Yes. That was it, exactly. And what about you?"

Miss Gray came to stand beside Josie. "I would claim I needed air as well, but I have the sense you would see through that assertion. In truth, I'm afraid I don't belong inside."

Josie wrinkled her brow. "Really? You seem like the sort of lady who would belong in any room she stumbled into."

"Me? Heavens no. I'm just the healer. Now, Lady Woodley is wonderfully kind and welcoming, of course, but I'm little better than a servant. If I wasn't always here, I doubt I would be involved in such family affairs."

Josie laughed. "You are always here because they like

you—they know you are the reason Lady Woodley lives."

Miss Gray pursed her lips. "But Lady Woodley is much improved. I am always here because—" She broke off. "No."

Josie leaned forward, her own feelings softened, at least for the moment, by her curiosity. "Why?"

Miss Gray looked over her shoulder, as if making sure they weren't being watched. "I'm here because Gabriel is...oh, he is the most frustrating man and he insists I keep returning."

Josie's eyes went wide. She had not expected that answer, but perhaps she should have. Evan had been rather distracted of late, which probably did leave his younger brother to keep up the household. And Gabriel was well known for his meticulous nature, after all.

"Does he?"

Miss Gray scowled. "Yes, he is always checking my work and wanting me to do things differently."

"*All* the Woodley men are terrible bothers, I assure you."

Miss Gray stared at her. "You include your fiancé in that statement?"

"Especially my fiancé," Josie laughed, though referring to Evan that way for the first time gave her a thrill. She shook her head. "What is your first name?"

"Juliet," Miss Gray offered.

"Josie," Josie returned. "And since we each seem to be tormented by Woodleys, I think we should be friends."

"I would like that."

Josie let out a long sigh before she spoke again. "Perhaps I shouldn't be so hard on the Woodley men. You know, Gabriel is actually a very decent fellow."

Juliet did not confirm or deny her own feelings on that subject. "And what of your fiancé?"

Josie stared out at the garden again. "More than decent. He is wonderful."

"Then why are you standing outside on the terrace with such a sad look in your eyes?" the healer asked softly.

Josie flitted her gaze toward her new friend. "Did I look

sad?"

"You do," Juliet said.

"You said you didn't belong inside," Josie said slowly. "I'm not certain I do either. I mean, look at Evan. He's devilishly handsome and he's very popular in the right crowds in London. I fear they are all looking at me and wondering why in the world he would choose me."

Juliet tilted her head and examined Josie closely. She shifted under the scrutiny and prayed Miss Gray wasn't asking the same question.

"Do you really not know?" she asked instead. "You can't see the way he looks at you?"

Josie's lips parted. "The way he looks at me?"

Juliet nodded as she said, "Oh yes. I noticed it at Lady Audrey's wedding when you first arrived the shire, and every time I have been in the room with you two I have noted the same. He is obviously very attracted to you. Do you really doubt that?"

Josie sighed as she thought of the way Evan touched her, kissed her and reassured her of her beauty. When he said it, she actually believed that it was true.

"I suppose I do know sometimes," she admitted with a blush. "But is it so obvious? Everyone else seemed shocked."

Juliet laughed softly. "I think it's harder for those close to us to see the change in people. I speak a great deal with Lady Woodley and she has told me you have been a friend to the family for a great many years. Especially to Claire. That is how they labeled you, so to see you take on a new role probably does surprise them. But if it helps, I didn't see it as an unpleasant surprise."

Josie smiled. Juliet had such a soothing way about her; she couldn't help but be reassured by her words.

"Thank you for listening to me," she said. "I know I sound a fool—"

Juliet shook her head. "Not in the slightest. I think most of us question our place every now and then, don't we?"

The terrace doors opened behind them and both women looked back to see who had joined them. Josie's heart leapt as she saw Evan step out onto the terrace, his eyes searching for her. When they settled on her, his gaze grew heavy-lidded, sensual.

Juliet patted her hand. "You know, I think I should check on Lady Woodley. This excitement will have to be monitored."

"Thank you again for your kind ear and support."

"It was my pleasure," Juliet said as she moved toward the house with a slight incline of her head for Evan. "My lord."

Once she had gone inside, Evan moved toward Josie slowly. "You have made a new friend."

She nodded. "I think I have. Juliet Gray is a very nice person, I can see why your mother likes her so much."

Evan reached out and suddenly his hand covered hers on the stone surface along the top of the low terrace wall. "If she helped you, then I like her too."

"Helped me?" Josie repeated, though her mouth went dry as he smoothed his hand back and forth against hers. The rhythmic touch was hypnotic and erotic at once.

"You slipped away from the crowd and I saw the look on your face. I would have come sooner to check on you, but I was detained by well-wishers."

Josie shifted and broke her gaze from his. "Am I so transparent?"

"Only to me, I suppose," he said. "You left because you were uncomfortable."

She almost denied his claim, almost shoved her emotions deep down inside where he wouldn't see them. But then she thought of what Juliet had said about him caring for her. She knew that to be true. It wasn't love. But it was something.

"I was a little," she admitted. "But now you are here and I find myself less so."

He smiled at that admission, and the hand covering hers lifted to touch her cheek instead. The desire she'd seen in his gaze when he first entered the terrace flared again and her body responded in kind.

"My mother tells me that Audrey and Jude have already departed London for their wedding trip and it is too far for them to come. But she believes Mary and Edward could join us by the weekend if the news is sent today," Evan said softly. "Once they arrive, we could marry any time after I obtain the special license."

Her heart leapt. "So soon?"

He nodded.

"But we don't have to rush," she said, trying to quell the returning anxiety that gripped her. "After all, no one knows the truth about why we were engaged so hastily."

His eyebrows lifted slightly. "No one but us," he corrected. "We know the truth."

She frowned. "Are you overcome by honor again, Evan?"

He barked out a laugh that made her jump in surprise. "God no," he said when he regained his composure. "The opposite, actually. You see, Josie, I don't think I could wait any longer to have you in my arms again. In my bed again. I want to be with you, so my reasons for hasty marriage are actually quite the opposite of honorable."

Her lips parted at that unexpected admission. Unexpected and entirely erotic as she thought about all the pleasure they would soon share.

"When we are married," she whispered, "There will be nothing hidden. Nothing denied."

"Nothing at all," he agreed, his voice almost a purr.

She leaned in closer and tilted her face toward his. "Then I utterly approve of this speedy union, my lord."

"Excellent," he chuckled before he slipped his fingers along her cheeks, tilted her face higher and pressed his lips to hers.

She expected the kiss to be passionate, as it had been when she agreed to be his bride, but Evan surprised her. His lips were gentle against hers, coaxing even though she freely gave. When his tongue finally slid out to trace the crease of her lips, she opened hungrily, but he did not devour. He seduced slowly and with finesse. And her knees shook at the idea that this was what he could do to her just as easily as sweep her off her feet.

She lifted her hands to grip his biceps as she lost herself in him for this moment in time. The love in her swelled and she found herself wishing it would never end. If they had passion, she had to hope that one day they might have more. And that once their wedding came and went, they would continue to grow the bond that had started in such wonderful and unexpected ways.

By the time Josie and her mother left, it was late. The house was beginning to grow quiet as Evan walked down the long, twisting hallways that led to the office Edward often used to handle estate business when he was here. Tonight Evan intended to use it to write a few letters to obtain his special license and inform people, including his staff in London, about his engagement.

As he opened the door to the room, he was surprised to find it not dark and quiet, but lit by a roaring fire, all the lamps blazing. When he entered the room, Gabriel rose from a chair beside the window.

"I thought you might come here," Gabriel said.

Evan barely stifled a sigh at the determined look on his brother's face. There seemed to be no escaping it.

"Good evening," he said as he stepped inside and shut the door behind himself. "I wondered where you'd gone. You were there for after-supper drinks with Josie and her mother and then you seemed to just vanish."

His brother's gaze darted away and Evan frowned. Gabriel was normally so direct, sometimes even to his detriment.

"What is it?" he pressed as he moved closer.

Gabriel shook his head. "I was simply ensuring Miss Gray

was taken home in a carriage. The woman wanted to walk home by moonlight, can you imagine? Why, it's almost two miles to her father's home. I had to argue with her for fifteen minutes before she would agree. She can truly be the most frustrating person."

"Ah," Evan said, confused by this subject. "I suppose I wouldn't know. I haven't spent a great deal of time talking to her about anything but Mama's care. And on that score, she seems very reasonable."

Gabriel muttered something under his breath but turned away and it was clear he did not want to pursue the subject further. So Evan turned to another one.

"Why didn't you return to the family?"

Gabriel faced him again and that guilty, cagey look was on his face again. "What?"

"After you dealt with your situation regarding Miss Gray, why didn't you return to the parlor?"

Gabriel shrugged. "I assumed the mothers were likely haranguing you and Josie with wedding details. I didn't feel like throwing myself on that particular pyre, so I took a walk by the lake instead."

Evan moved to the sideboard behind Edward's desk and poured two glasses of scotch. When he handed one over to Gabriel, his brother did not refuse.

"Well, you were not wrong in your assessment," Evan said as he sat down in a chair beside fire. Gabriel joined him. "They are thrilled about the marriage, of course. And since we are rushing to do this, they have many details to plan."

"I can't believe you're doing it at all, let alone rushing it."

Evan frowned. "But you know why. You are the only one who knows why aside from Josie and myself."

"Yes, I've been thinking about that since last night," Gabriel said, steepling his fingers together. "Why did you let things go so far?"

Evan stared at the leaping flames before him and pondered the question. "When I began with Josie, you said I knew the line between flirtation and seduction. But it turns out I didn't. At least not with her."

"But why?" Gabriel asked.

Evan wrinkled his brow. "Haven't you ever been with a woman you couldn't resist? Felt so much desire that it overcame reason?"

Gabriel pinched his lips. "I never lose my grip on reason."

"I suppose I should say that is lucky," Evan said with a sigh. "But I don't think it is. There is something to be said for desire so powerful that it means more than breath. With wanting another person so much that you would be willing to give up everything to be with her."

"That sounds like more than simply losing your reason," Gabriel said with an incredulous look.

Evan stared at his clenched hands in his lap. "Perhaps it is more."

He said the words out loud and he felt how real they were. Oh, he had already admitted he *cared* for Josie. But he cared for a lot of people. No, what he felt for the woman who would be his wife was something a great deal more. He wasn't ready to name it yet, though. Once he named that feeling, it would be very, very powerful.

And he wasn't ready.

Gabriel tilted his head to look at him more closely and Evan felt the hawkishness of his younger brother's intelligent stare.

"Why do you look at me that way?" he grunted.

Gabriel shrugged. "I was just thinking that once you are married, you will have access to your wife's things. Her letters."

Evan lifted his gaze slowly and caught Gabriel's. The same thought had flitted through his own mind, as well, but hearing it stated out loud made it feel...*cruel.*

"You think I should go digging through Josie's private things in order to uncover information about Claire?" he asked.

"Of course," Gabriel said with a huff of breath. "When

else will we have the chance to look at what Claire wrote to her best friend?"

Evan shook his head. "God, do you hear yourself? You want me to violate my wife's privacy within, what, the first moments of our union."

"No!" Gabriel burst out. "I thought perhaps a few hours. She'll sleep at some point on your wedding night and—"

"God, I hope not," Evan muttered.

His brother ignored him and pushed to his feet with a frustrated breath. "If you aren't intending to uncover any information about Claire, then what was all this for? Why did you approach Josie in the first place? Was seduction for nothing? Did you throw away your life to marry her for nothing?"

"No," Evan said the word firmly. "I want you to hear me. My initial approach of Josie may well have been because I suspected she knew something about our sister. But that ceased to be my purpose long ago. And I can't use her, Gabriel. I won't."

Gabriel groaned. The sound was low and animal and filled with such agony that Evan flinched. He stared up at Gabriel. His brother's face was twisted in such pain, such loss that Evan felt sorry for him. Gabriel was desperate to save Claire. Desperate enough to do *anything*. And he couldn't understand why everyone else around him didn't feel the same.

"I want to help you," Evan said, standing and moving toward his brother. "God knows I want to help Claire. But I'm not certain that what you want me to do is going to do anything at all to find her or assist her."

Gabriel spun away. "And so you refuse to try. Even a little."

Evan scrubbed a hand over his face. "God damn it, Gabriel. I'm not abandoning Claire. When Josie is more comfortable, when she's ready, I will ask her again what our sister said to her."

"So in a month or six months or a year," Gabriel said with

a shake of his head. "And what if that is too late?"

Evan flinched. "Don't say that."

"I must say it. It is the image that runs through my mind every moment of every day!" Gabriel shouted, his face suddenly red and his eyes wild. "Our sister dead at the hands of that bastard who took her. And we did nothing. We did nothing to save her."

"I'm not doing nothing," Evan whispered.

Gabriel barked out a laugh that was harsh in the quiet room. "We'll keep telling ourselves that, shall we? Congratulations on your engagement, brother. Good night."

With that Gabriel stormed from the room, leaving Evan to ponder all the ugly things he had said. And all the fears he had never allowed himself to face.

CHAPTER SIXTEEN

In the end, it took over a week, but as Josie stood before the mirror in Audrey's old chamber at the Woodley home, she saw the reflection of a wife. She was married.

"Here, let us remove the veil," Juliet offered as she gently slipped the pins from the piece. "You will be more comfortable in just the gown during the gathering."

"Thank you," Josie whispered to her new friend, and saw Juliet smile warmly at her in the mirror reflection.

Behind Josie stood her own mother alongside Lady Woodley, Mrs. Samson, Jude's mother, Mary and Mary's sister Gemma. All of them beamed without hesitation.

And though Josie was now married to the man she loved, *she* felt hesitation. Oh, Evan had been attentive since their engagement and even passionate if they could steal a kiss in a corridor, but she had also felt a change in him. A wariness she couldn't explain and didn't like.

What if he regretted this choice? Right now he might be able to hide it, but as his passion for her faded, she feared he would begin to resent her.

"You are gorgeous, Josie," Gemma said with a happy smile that drew her from her worries.

Though Josie had only met the wife of the notorious Crispin Flynn a few days ago, she already liked her immensely. She had the same kindness that her younger sister did. And her husband, though very dashing, was not quite the rogue rumor had implied he would be.

Mary nodded. "Gemma is right. You practically glow. Evan couldn't keep his eyes off of you all through the ceremony!"

Josie blushed at the compliments that actually eased her fears a little. "Thank you, Mary, Gemma. I must admit, in this dress, I actually feel...*pretty*."

She looked at herself again and how the creamy fabric of her gown fell over her often-hated curves. But the seamstress who had made the gown was not her usual choice, but one Lady Woodley hired from town, and the young woman had a flair for making the fashions of the day look wonderful even on a body that did not fit them.

"You *are* very pretty," Lady Woodley said, rising from the chair where she had been ordered by Juliet to rest and coming through the group to stand beside Josie.

Josie smiled at her. Her new mother-in-law put her so to mind of the Woodley children. They all shared her eyes and the brightness of their smiles. And now Josie was one of them, a Woodley.

"My son seems very happy today, Josie," Lady Woodley continued as she smoothed an errant curl away from Josie's forehead. "And Claire..."

She trailed off and for a moment the room became silent, heavy. Josie reached out to grasp Lady Woodley's hand and her new mother-in-law squeezed it gently.

"Oh, Claire would have loved this!" Lady Woodley finally whispered with only a slight crack to her voice.

"I miss her too," Josie said softly, and they stood together for a few seconds, pondering their loss on this day of happiness.

Then Lady Woodley shook her head. "Oh, and Audrey! I know she is very sorry to miss this day."

"I don't begrudge her this wedding trip, I assure you," Josie said with a smile. Now that she had experienced passion, she actually was jealous of the secluded cabin by the sea that

Audrey was currently sharing with her handsome husband, Jude Samson. "I got a letter from her this morning, a lovely letter. Though she said you must each promise to write to her and tell her all the details of today so she can live vicariously through you."

Lady Woodley laughed. "And I'm sure as soon as you are all back in London next week, my daughter will call on you and demand to hear them again."

"I hope so," Josie said with a smile. "I look forward to seeing her."

"We have been up here for a while," Juliet said softly. "Perhaps we should return to the party?"

Josie cast a glance at herself in the mirror once more. "Yes. I am ready to face the world and my husband once more."

But as the rest moved toward the door, Josie stayed in her spot for a moment and drew a long breath. Downstairs Evan awaited her and she could only hope she would see only good things in his stare when she came into view.

Evan looked up the stairs as the gaggle of women came giggling and chatting downward. His heart leapt for he knew that meant Josie would be close behind. As the women scattered at the bottom of the stairs, they no longer blocked her descent—and there *she* was.

All day he had been taken aback by her presence, her beauty, and this moment was no different. He sucked in a breath, his knees going weak at the sight of her. And when she met his gaze and smiled…he was lost.

He moved toward her almost like he was in a dream and reached out a hand. She took it as she finished her descent, her fingers tightening against his, and looked up at him with a smile.

"Hello."

He almost laughed at that one little word. So simple, so benign, and yet her voice hit him in the gut, wound up in him, tightened around his heart.

"You took far too long," he murmured as he lifted her hand to his lips and felt the cool metal band on her finger that signified she was his for all time.

"Did I?" she asked with a gasp of panic. "Oh, were people asking about me, did—"

"Not people," he interrupted. "*Me.* I swear it felt like you were gone an eternity."

She blushed at his words, but she didn't dip her head or look away. "Oh," she said softly. "Well, how can I make it up to you?"

He laughed at the innocence and wickedness that combined in that question. "I will show you later. For now, you may start by sharing this dance with me, wife."

She shifted and he saw her gaze slip through the ballroom doors. "I-I am not a very good dancer," she whispered, as if that admission were the most embarrassing in the world.

He smiled as he slid her hand into the crook of his arm and guided her into the ballroom. All eyes turned to look at them, and dancers stepped back as they made their way onto the floor. He saw Josie's panic flare and squeezed her hand.

"Don't worry," he whispered. "I will lead and you follow. In this, at least, I know what I'm doing."

She smiled at the quip, and as the music swelled, he guided her into the steps of their first dance together. At first she moved a little awkwardly, as if she knew the steps but hadn't performed them for a very long time. He supposed that was true, for she had admitted as much to him before. But he kept his gaze on her, adjusted her gently if she went astray, and soon she swung to the music as if she had been made for dancing. Or at least dancing with him.

Everything else around them faded. The wedding guests, their families, the orchestra, the ballroom...all that was left was the two of them, her in his arms, together at last.

He could have remained that way forever, but the music faded and the sounds of those around them clapping broke the spell between them. They stopped moving and she blushed as she ducked her head. Around them the crowd tittered, and he thought he heard someone whisper loudly, "Perhaps it is a love match after all."

He ignored it all except to nod to the crowd and then guide his bride away. Soon more couples flooded the space they had left and everyone went back to their drinks and gossip.

He guided Josie away through the room and out onto the terrace where they could have a moment alone. Their first since declared husband and wife that afternoon.

She smiled up at him as he came to a stop at the edge of the terrace. "We seem to have a habit of ending up alone on terraces."

He lifted his eyebrows suggestively. "I arrange for that, you know."

Her laughter seemed to lighten the tension in her and when she stopped she said, "Thank you for the dance."

"You are most welcome," he responded. "But you were not truthful with me earlier. You said you were not a good dancer."

She blushed. "It seems I only needed the right partner."

Evan took a slight step away from her and looked out into the night. Josie meant she had the right partner on the floor, but in his mind he had begun to wonder if he had indeed found the right partner in life. Despite their odd beginning.

"Have I done something wrong?" Josie asked softly.

He jerked his gaze to find her looking up at him, green eyes wide and wild, her jaw set as if she assumed she would hear bad news and wanted to be ready for it.

"Wrong? No, why?" he asked.

She swallowed hard. "It is only that over the past few days, since we announced our engagement to our families, I have felt your...distance. Sometimes you seem very pensive."

He opened his mouth to speak, but she held up a hand. "Evan, I realize that our marriage is not exactly how you would have chosen your future. I accept that. But I don't want your resentments to fester over time and destroy any happiness or comfort we could find together. So I hope you'll be honest with me."

Her words, meant to make him open up, only made his frown deeper.

Be honest with her?

If only she knew that was exactly why he had been holding back. He knew he had started their connection with a lie. Just one, but one that would hurt her deeply. That lie was that he had meant to use her.

And one day he would tell her that. But not now. Not when she was so raw about it. Not when it might make her turn away.

He took her hand. "The night we announced the engagement, I had a row with Gabriel."

She blinked. "Another argument? What was it over?"

"It's not important," he said, again not wanting to broach a subject that might cause her pain on a day when she should be happy. "But my discord with my brother is likely what you picked up on since."

She nodded slowly and he breathed a sigh of relief. At least he didn't have to lie completely. His argument with his brother *had* been a source of discomfort. Only it was because Evan was torn between Gabriel's desire for him to find out more from Josie and Evan's true feelings for her. He was tormented by their original plan to use her attraction against her.

He didn't feel good about those actions.

"It isn't you," he promised.

"Good," she whispered. "I was worried. I couldn't tell what you were thinking."

"You needn't," he said. "And right now I am thinking about our wedding night."

She let out a light, nervous laugh. "It *is* our wedding night."

"No, this is our wedding party," he corrected as he took her hand again and drew her a bit closer. "In a few hours, when we go back to your mother's house and are almost entirely alone—"

"Actually," she interrupted. "We will be entirely alone. While we were upstairs, your mother invited my mother to stay here for the night so that we could have privacy."

"Oh, that is even better," he murmured, unable to keep his mind from spinning wicked, wicked scenarios. "All right, then tonight when we are alone, I plan to do such things to you, wife."

She swallowed hard, but he could see desire in her eyes. It brightened her expression and dilated her pupils.

"Like what?" she whispered, her voice rough.

"If you make me say it, then I'll have to show you." His tone was suddenly low and rough, even though he laughed.

Her breath hitched in primal response. "What's wrong with that?"

"You are a minx, do you know that? A temptress."

She joined in his laughter even though her eyes went wide. "I don't think anyone has ever called me that before. Shall I take it as a compliment or a curse?"

"A bit of both," he said, drawing her closer yet again. "You make me wild with wanting you, all I can think of is you. But if I tell you all the ways I want to touch you and taste you and claim you, I will be forced to either have you against that wall right there." He pointed to a shadowy portion of the terrace. "Or I will have to walk around for the remainder of the party with a very obvious, er, show of my desire for you."

For a moment she appeared confused, but then she glanced down with a pointed look at his cock. Which of course went harder with her attention.

"Oh—oh!" she gasped, her cheeks pinkening. "Oh, goodness, I see."

"So we should probably go inside, yes?" he said with a laugh.

She nodded. "That would be best. Only I would like to do something first."

"What is that?"

She didn't answer with words, but instead lifted to her tiptoes, cupped his cheeks and brushed her lips against his. He was surprised by the sweetness of the action, but surprise quickly turned to increased desire when her tongue darted out to gently trace the crease of his lips. He brought his arms around her, using all his control not to crush her to his chest, and opened his mouth to her explorations. The kiss deepened as she tilted her head, granting better access and finding it with that one movement. When they had stood kissing for what seemed like forever, she let out a little moan deep in her throat.

Their lips broke, though he continued to hold her close. She smiled. "So sorry, my lord."

"Why?" he panted.

She arched her hips a little and he grunted at the contact of her pelvis with his now very erect cock. "That. It seems I *am* a curse."

She grinned as she said it and he couldn't help but smile back at this new, relaxed Josie. He rather liked this side of her, light and free, comfortable with him and their desire for each other.

He couldn't wait to explore her further.

"A terrible curse," he teased back, "who should go back inside before she is thoroughly mussed herself."

He set her aside, turned her toward the door and gave her a swat on her curvaceous backside. She yelped in surprise, but he thought a little pleasure as she looked at him over her shoulder. "And what will *you* do?"

"Stand here with my back to the door and do a recitation of each and every governess, tutor and professor I ever had. And hope that distraction will make me presentable soon." He gave her a playful glare. "Go, woman! Go!"

She giggled as she did as she had been told, disappearing into the house and back into the party. When she was gone, he turned his attention back to the darkness of the garden and the duty to ease his desire.

"Nanny Plum, the old goat," he began as he smiled up at the full moon. "Nanny Jane, rest her soul…"

Josie all but danced back into the ballroom, her heart soaring. If she had been nervous about Evan's thoughts about her before, those few stolen moments on the terrace had eased her fears. He wanted her. More than that, he *liked* her.

Oh, she had known that, she supposed. But now it meant a great deal more to her. She could picture their life together, laid out before them. And what she saw was years of playful in-jokes, laughter and passion, so much passion.

Eventually, he might even come to love her. Why not? They had a good base on which to build such a powerful connection.

She smiled at her guests and was about to rejoin the mothers and Mary across the room when Gabriel came into her view. He was standing beside the refreshment table, a drink in his hand. And he was watching her.

She cast a glance toward the terrace. Evan hadn't yet come back inside, but she thought of what he'd said to her earlier. A row with his brother had set him on his heels the past few days. And wasn't part of her job as wife to help smooth these things over?

She took a deep breath, for she wasn't comfortable with such things, and crossed the room to her new brother-in-law. As she reached him, she smiled.

"Good evening, Gabriel."

He had watched her approach, but Gabriel actually seemed surprised to hear her voice. "Oh yes, hello, Josie."

Her brow knitted at the slight slur to his tone and the glassiness of his gaze. "Gabriel, are you...are you drunk?" she whispered in shock.

It wasn't so much that the concept was shocking in general. Men drank—it was practically a national pastime for those of their rank. But Gabriel *didn't*. She recalled Claire making specific note of how her twin always stayed in control of his faculties, limited his alcohol intake to one drink every so often.

He blinked as if digesting her words. "Drunk? Indeed, it appears so," he said with a slight bow. "Are you?"

She smiled as she reached out to pat his arm. "No, not this time."

"Would you like to be? I could fetch you a drink." He motioned behind him where a strong punch was within reach. "'Tis no trouble, I assure you."

"I appreciate the offer," Josie said. "But I think not."

He shrugged. "Suit yourself. Did you only come to see me out of control? It's a sight, they say, rarely seen. Museum quality."

He teased her, but in his eyes she saw a darkness. A sadness. And she thought of Claire and frowned. Her friend wouldn't want her most beloved brother to be in such pain.

"Gabriel, Evan tells me you two argued around the time of our engagement," she said softly, watching his face closely. "I hope it wasn't over me."

Gabriel hiccupped. "Of course it was over you. What else would we argue about?"

Josie flinched. When their engagement was announced, Gabriel had been kind enough, but his welcoming had obviously been for show. Now without a filter, he was showing his true hesitations.

"I realize it was fast, Gabriel, but I assure you that I will make the best bride I can for Evan. And I will prove myself to you. Just don't punish him for your hesitations about me. I know it hurts him."

Gabriel stared at her, his brow wrinkling with confusion. "Hesitations about you? God no. You're fine. He seems to like you well enough. After all, he won't do what I want. If he didn't like you, why would he care? Why wouldn't he just do it?"

Josie shook her head. "I—what?"

"It's not about you," Gabriel said slowly, enunciating each words and rolling his eyes as if she were daft. "Well, it *is*, but not how you think."

Josie felt like the room was spinning even though she wasn't the one who was drunk. She didn't know what the hell Gabriel was talking about, but anxiety was beginning to knot in her stomach regardless.

"What is it then?" she asked softly. "About me but not about me."

He was silent for what seemed like forever. "Claire," he finally choked out. "Everything is always about Claire. But he won't help. He won't do what needs to be done. So she's lost. Lost, Josie."

He was blinking rapidly and she could see he was choking on high emotion. She reached out to touch his hand this time and squeezed gently. "Oh, Gabriel. I know it hurts you deeply. We *all* love her and miss her."

"But not enough," he grunted. "Not enough to make the hard choices. To do the distasteful things. Not him. Not you."

He shook off her hand and, without another word, walked away. She watched him go, helpless and still confused by his insistence that somehow Evan wasn't willing to help with Claire. She had no idea what Gabriel wanted Evan to do or whatever that could have to do with her.

But she could see now what Evan had gone through with his brother recently. Gabriel was still deep in his pain, even though Claire had been gone nearly two years. And after talking to him for five minutes she wanted desperately to help him, so she could only imagine how Evan felt.

Perhaps once things had settled down, they could work

together to ease some of Gabriel's pain. Or even work on finding Claire and bringing her home.

"Jocelyn?"

She turned at her name and found Mary standing there, a smile on her face. "Yes?"

"Lord and Lady Trefeld are about to depart and were looking to say goodbye. I cannot seem to find Evan anywhere, so will you join Edward and me in saying the farewells?"

Josie nodded and followed Mary across the room. She was just as happy for the interruption. Thoughts of Claire and the confusing conversation with Gabriel were islands of sadness on this otherwise happy day.

And if she was lucky, it was about to lead to a wonderful night as well.

CHAPTER SEVENTEEN

Josie could hardly hear over the rush of blood in her ears, and her hands shook as she parted them from their grip in front of her to allow her maid to lift her dressing gown over her shoulders. Nell smoothed the fabric a few times and then knotted a pretty bow at Josie's waist with the robe ties.

She stepped back. "You look lovely, ma'am."

Josie shifted slightly and glanced at herself in the mirror. Nell had brought her dark hair down and fluffed and combed it until the soft waves shone. Her cheeks were pink with nervousness and her eyes wide.

"This room feels very small right now," she whispered, her voice rough.

Nell laughed. "Well, normally we have the dressing room door open to your chamber. But since your husband awaits you there and we closed the door, it does make the room feel small. Is there anything else I can do for you?"

Josie swallowed hard, her throat suddenly full and thick with worry. "I—no," she stammered.

"Then I'll step out," Nell said, moving to the door that led to Josie's private sitting room rather than her bedchamber. "Good luck, my lady."

Luck. Josie shut her eyes as her maid left her alone. She didn't need luck. After all, her virginity was already gone. But that had been done in a sweeping moment of passion and demand. It had been hurried by circumstance and location.

Tonight would be different. Tonight she and Evan were alone in the house aside from a few key servants. They were wedded and would not be interrupted. Tonight she was a wife, and this time when Evan took her, it would be more than just a thoughtless claim. It was a promise of a future.

More than that, she had come to realize she loved him. And the binding of their bodies now meant so very much more to her.

"Oh God," she muttered beneath her breath as she stared at the barrier between her and her bedchamber. "Just open the door."

She reached out her trembling hand and caught the door handle. With a whispered prayer, she turned it and pushed, slowly revealing her bedchamber.

She had been expecting to see it as it usually was. The way it had been her entire life. But when she stepped inside, it was like coming into an entirely different place. While she had been readying her body for this night, Evan had also been busy preparing her room.

Candles were lit all around, giving the chamber a soft glow, and her fire burned brightly. Her room smelled of roses, and she saw why. Evan had scattered the petals all around the bed and on a path leading to it.

But the thing that drew her attention most, that made this the most special of evenings, was the man himself. He stood beside the fire, his shirt already removed, his feet bare, and he just *stared* at her.

"You are beautiful with your hair down," he breathed.

She lifted her hand to the tresses. "I suppose, despite it all, you have never seen it like this."

"No. We were always too hurried, too focused on other things, too afraid of being caught to take it down. But now that I see you this way, I want to keep you like this forever."

"In my night clothes with my hair around my shoulders?" she said, her laughter rusty and rough with the desire building in her.

He nodded. "And ready for me."

"I am very ready," she whispered. "Though slightly terrified."

He cocked his head. "Really? Why terrified?" Then understanding dawned. "Oh, Josie, the first time, the pain, that will never happen again."

"No, it isn't the pain that frightens me. Honestly, I have not thought of the pain once since that night, and I have dreamed of our stolen moment a hundred times."

He swallowed hard. "Then what?"

"You won't be swept away by passion tonight," she whispered. "And I don't want to disappoint you."

He smiled and finally took a few steps toward her. She felt his heat even before he touched her, dragging the back of his hand across her cheek. "I will most definitely be swept away by passion before this night is through. And I already know you could never disappoint me."

Then he bent his head, and any words she might have said evaporated. His lips were gentle at first, brushing hers with whisper-light pressure. But when she lifted her hands to his biceps, gripping the muscle there to remain steady, the ardor in his kiss increased. He cupped the back of her head, drawing her closer, angling her as he dipped his tongue inside and thoroughly explored her mouth.

Her knees went weak and her body woke in that wonderful way she had come to expect since the first time he touched her. Her nipples began to tingle, her thighs parted without hesitation and inside the wetness and warmth of her sex increased. He did this to her with ease, without even trying overly hard at it.

And this was just the beginning.

She turned her face, breaking the kiss, and he leaned away to look down at her.

"What's wrong?" he asked, his voice low and hypnotic.

"Nothing," she gasped. "I just needed breath."

"I know the feeling," he muttered. "Though I rather like taking your breath away, Josie. I intend to do it over and over tonight. Until you forget everything in the world but me and us."

She glided one hand from his bicep to his shoulder and then down his chest, tracing the muscles on her route. "I already do," she murmured.

He dipped his head and kissed her once more. But this time he didn't merely kiss. His fingers danced along her sides to the knot of her robe. With a flick of his wrist, he undid the pretty precision of Nell's bow and parted the garment. He stepped back as he slid it away and looked at her.

She blushed. This was her prettiest chemise. It was pale blue with fine stitching and soft fabric. It clung to her curves, just as all her clothing did, but for the first time she felt no self-consciousness of that fact.

Because she knew Evan liked her body. It made her more confident about her appearance and she found herself arching her back a little, letting her breasts entice him.

He grumbled out a curse below his breath before he caught the strap of her chemise and tugged. The feather-soft silk glided down her body, catching on the fullness of her hips before a second gentle tug from him made it pool at her feet.

She had been naked with him before, of course. In the cottage, the second time he had brought her pleasure. But tonight it felt…different. Because she was his now. This wasn't as stolen moment, but an important one. It marked the next chapter in the book of their life together.

And she trembled as he stared at her.

"I've dreamt of you like this for weeks," he admitted, cupping one breast gently, dragging his thumb back and forth over the peak. "And my memory was not as good as reality."

She blushed at the compliment. "I've dreamt of you as well," she admitted. "And wanted you so desperately."

"Then let us both have our dream come true, shall we?" He dropped his hand from her, a fact that would have troubled her if he hadn't swiftly unfastened his trousers instead. He pushed them away, and now they were both naked.

"You are so beautiful, Evan," she murmured. "So wonderfully perfect."

He arched an eyebrow. "Isn't that what I'm meant to say?"

"Don't tease," she said, dragging her fingers across his chest again, but this time going lower, to his stomach, the trail of wiry hair that guided her to his cock. "I'm not."

"I wouldn't be so certain," he grunted as she took him in hand and stroked him gently. He was already so hard, so ready, and she wanted him to be inside her. She wanted him to take her, to claim her, to be hers at last.

He bent his head to kiss her and broke her hand away as he swept his arm beneath her knees. He lifted her and swallowed her yelp of surprise as he carried her to the bed. He laid her across the pillows, her hair spread around her like a fan, and climbed up beside her to roll on his side.

As he continued to kiss her until she was weak and spinning, his hands smoothed over her. He cupped her breast again, teasing and tormenting her nipple with his questing fingers until she arched against him with a strangled moan.

He chuckled without breaking their kiss and slid his hand lower, leaving a tingling path in his wake. He smoothed the skin of her hip, then touched her thigh. Her legs parted and he took the invitation of her body and cupped her sex.

Her gasp broke their kiss and she looked up at him through a bleary gaze. "What do you do to me?" she murmured as the pleasure of his touch increased. He massaged her sex, thumbing her clitoris and gliding her body's wetness over her rhythmically.

"I want to do everything," he growled as he rolled to cover her.

She gasped with pleasure as he settled between her thighs, his naked flesh pressed head to toe to hers at last. The hardness of his erection nudged the softness of her aching slit and she lifted her hips to rub against him in an effort to find relief at last.

"Don't rush," he murmured as his mouth covered hers

again. "We have all night."

She moaned at the thought of this torment all night. Of being so ready, so willing, so filled with desire and having him draw out the waiting. She just might combust.

She lifted her hips again and his cock slid along her entrance a second time. He grunted with pleasure and pulled away from her lips.

"You do not listen well, do you, Josie?"

"I just want you so much," she admitted. "Fast and hard, slow and steady, it doesn't matter. Just don't make me wait anymore."

He nodded and positioned himself differently. She felt the head of him now, pressed to her entrance, pushing in instead of across. Slowly he eased forward and she opened to him readily, accepting his length, his girth, his everything. She waited for the pain, but found he was correct. Unlike in the parlor the week before, there was none. Only stretching fullness and awakening nerves.

He fully seated himself deep within her and let out a shuddering sigh. "At last," he murmured.

"Yes," she agreed, holding him closer, their bodies as one. She was his in every way now. Her heart swelled with love for him even as her body ached for more.

And as if he sensed her second thought, he began to move. Unlike the first time, where everything had been fast and blurry, Evan went slowly. He guided back, letting her feel the full length of him, then rolled forward. Their pelvises ground together with the action, her clitoris stimulated by the rocking of his hips.

He repeated the motion as he claimed her mouth, driving his tongue in time to his cock. She melted away under his care, her entire focus becoming the press of their bodies, the rub of his skin on hers. She found herself lifting to him, meeting his thrusts with ones of her own, and soon their rhythm was the same. Take and give, press and retreat, building toward the crescendo of pleasure she felt building deep between her thighs.

It came on slowly, rising with promise until she dug her nails into his shoulders, silently pleading for relief from the mounting sensations.

He drew back from her lips and met her eyes instead. "Come for me, Josie," he whispered, his voice rough. "Let me see you."

His growled words were enough to push her over the edge, and she let out a keening cry as the pleasure washed over her in never-ending waves. She bucked beneath him, breaking the smooth cadence of their bodies. Not that it seemed to matter. As she cried out his name, his threw his head back, the tendons in his neck straining. He roared out his own pleasure and she felt the hot splash of his seed deep within her.

He collapsed against her still twitching body, holding to her like she was a lifeline. She smoothed his hair, pressing kisses to his neck as her pleasure faded away.

"Amazing," he murmured, his voice muffled before he rolled away to his side, dragging her against him.

She looked up his body. "Which part?"

"All of it," he said. "You. Us. It is unlike anything I've ever experienced before."

She sat up slightly to stare at him. "You cannot mean that."

"Ah, doubting me already," he said as he reached up to curl a lock of her hair around his finger.

She shook her head, refusing to be distracted. "Evan, you have been with women before. Many, if gossip is to be believed."

He frowned. "I was no monk before, no. Though I was no libertine."

"Either way, you've been with women of experience, ones who knew what to do, what to say, how to be."

He leaned up and cupped the back of her neck, drawing her close. As the heat of his breath warmed her lips, he said, "None of them was you. Do not doubt yourself, Josie. You most definitely know what to do, to say, to be when it comes to me. And I do not lie when I say that no one has ever made me burn more, want more, need more."

"Evan—" she began in further protest, but he silenced her by dropping his mouth to hers even as he cupped one breast. Pleasure overtook her again, passion he could both extinguish and ignite in the same breath.

And she didn't speak again, didn't think again until the fire had burned low and they were both spent.

CHAPTER EIGHTEEN

Evan glanced over at the outline of Josie's sleeping body. In the dying firelight, her skin looked even more like porcelain. Except it wasn't. She was real and warm and he had made her his so many times that night. A night of new beginnings.

But as he watched her smile gently in her sleep, he was troubled. His thoughts had been so jumbled since talking to Gabriel the day of his engagement. In truth, even before that.

He'd started down this road with Josie only to find out what she knew about Claire. Of course things had become more complicated. Emotions had become involved even if he hadn't wanted them to. But Gabriel's words hung in his ears. Taunted and tormented him. Was his brother right? Was he abandoning his lost sister just for his own pleasure?

He pushed out of the bed and found his discarded trousers on the floor beside it. Quietly he tugged them on, and then he paced to the fire to toss a log onto the dying flames. They rose slowly, brightening the room that had gone dim when the candles burned down.

He looked around. This was Josie's private room. It was filled with her things, knickknacks and clothing and jewelry that said she belonged there, rather than him. They were only sharing it because it was their wedding night. He supposed he could make a case now that they were man and wife that all these little things of hers were now his, including any correspondence between Josie and Claire, but he had never been that kind of domineering man. His father had never forced his mother to report her every move, and he wouldn't like it if Audrey were asked to do so. Why should he do that to his own wife?

But Claire...it always came back to Claire.

Claire was out there somewhere. And the few reports they had on her told him that she was being misused in far worse ways than merely having her privacy compromised.

"Damn it," he murmured.

What if he never had another chance to search these rooms? Tomorrow they would not stay here, perhaps they never would again. What if Gabriel was right that if he didn't do this tonight, right now, that Claire might...might...he couldn't even think it. It was too horrible to ponder. But if he searched Josie's chamber tonight and found some evidence, *could* he save Claire?

He found himself gently sliding open the drawer on Josie's bedside table. Inside was only a book and a stub of a candle, which he took and lit to guide him.

He hated himself for doing this. But he knew he would hate himself tenfold more if his sister was harmed because he hadn't. With a sigh, he crept to the opposite side of Josie's bed and found nothing of more interest in the other table.

He looked around the room again. He doubted she kept much correspondence here. There wasn't a good space to respond to letters. He looked to the connecting dressing room that Josie had stepped from in all her bridal glory just a few hours before. He shivered as he recalled that moment when she'd entered the chamber with her hands shaking in anticipation.

In that moment he'd been so proud to call her his.

And to reward her, he slipped into her dressing area and betrayed her by looking around. Gowns were hung on racks in the tiny room, and her wardrobe was along one wall with likely even more clothing inside. There was a table there, but it wasn't a desk. From the bottles and brushes lined up along the top, he thought this was likely where her maid did her hair each day. He could almost picture Josie sitting here, smiling and chatting while she was prepared for her activities. He suddenly wanted to watch that transformation.

He shook his head. That wasn't why he was snooping through her chambers. There was another door here. He pushed it open and found it led to a small, private sitting room. There wasn't much to it, really. Just a pair of chairs before an empty fireplace, a bookcase—and there, across the room, an escritoire.

He lifted his candle and moved to the little writing desk, his heart throbbing. As he set the candle on its surface, he found himself praying that there would be nothing noteworthy inside. That Josie had left any letters from his sister in London. Then he could report back to Gabriel that he had searched but found nothing. It would buy him time to decide how to handle the situation once they had returned to the city.

He opened the top drawer of the desk slowly and found it to contain only materials for letters. Paper, ink, a quill. He slid it shut and moved on to the second, deeper drawer. It squeaked a little as he opened it and he flinched at the accusatory sound. But he didn't stop. He couldn't now. The sin was already committed, now he had to finish what he'd started.

Inside the drawer were letters. He stared at the small stack, bound with a ribbon. He reached out to take the pile and tugged the bow loose. The finer point of how he had loosened another bow a few hours before, on Josie's robe was not lost on him. The first had been for pleasure, the second, disloyalty.

He leaned in closer to the light to examine the first letter. It was from her oldest brother. He put it aside, face down so he would remember the order when he put everything back. The second letter was from a friend, but not Claire, and he added it to the stack. A third was from her sister. His heart both soared and sank with each successive failure to find anything from Claire. Soared because he didn't have to commit the ultimate act of treachery and sank because he had no information to draw him closer to his wayward sister.

He turned past another letter that was of no interest to him, and froze. There on the next folded piece of thick vellum was Claire's handwriting. He would have known it anywhere even though there was no name on the outer sheet aside from Josie's. His breath hitched as he turned the paper over and broke the seal. There were two sheets within. He sat with the letter in his lap, staring at it.

There were his sister's words, meant not for him but for the best friend she loved and trusted. The same friend who cared for him and trusted him. Reading what was not meant for him was a violation of both women, but Gabriel's words rang in his ears. Was he willing to do anything to save Claire? Images of her being hurt jumped before his eyes, and he unfolded the sheets and began to read.

He had gotten no further than the greeting and the date of six months ago when he heard a shallow gasp behind him. He squeezed his eyes shut. He didn't need to look to know who had found him here.

"Evan!" Josie burst out, her voice shaking.

He set the letter aside and stood. Taking a deep breath, he turned to face his wife. She had put her robe back on and tied it loosely, but he could see the outline of her naked curves beneath the silk. With her hair mussed by sleep and passion, she made quite a lovely sight. One he might have had the opportunity to cherish.

Except that the betrayal in her eyes was already bright as she stared at him and the pile of her private correspondence on her desk.

"What are you doing?" she asked, her tone flat and pained.

He swallowed. "Josie—"

She shook her head as if in disbelief. "What are you doing, Evan?"

He could have lied in that moment. A dozen stories filled his head, ways to make that look of pain and betrayal leave her face. But Josie was too smart, and to lie to her would only sport with her intelligence. It would only make the situation worse.

"You—you told me you had received letters from my sister," he admitted. "I thought perhaps I would find some of them here."

Her lips parted as his words sank in and he watched her face go from confused to angry to betrayed to heartbroken in a flash of horror that made his stomach hurt.

"You left our wedding night bed to search through my *private* things."

Her words were not a question, but he answered her anyway. "Yes."

She blinked at him, looking at him like she had never seen him before. That expression stabbed him, and he moved toward her as if he could make her see that nothing had changed.

"How could you?" she asked, her voice soft but trembling. "Why? Why would this be your focus on our wedding night? Why would you want to—"

She stopped herself suddenly and her gaze jerked to his face again. Her mouth twisted and tears filled her eyes. Tears she blinked away before she spoke again.

"Was this why you pursued me, Evan? To get closer to the truth about Claire?"

He opened and shut his mouth a few times, trying to find an answer, but apparently his silence was a good enough response, for she spun away from him, staggering back through the dressing room and into the bedroom. He followed her in a few long strides.

"Wait, Josie, listen to me."

She pivoted to face him. "What is there to say, Evan? How stupid was I? I believed you when you said this wasn't your goal. I believed you even though you asked me about your sister several times when you spent time with me. I pretended it was because she was a common bond between us, that you needed a friend to hear your fears. But no, of course that wasn't it." She shook her head. "How foolish was I to believe I was your confidante? You only wanted me to tell you what I knew.

And you would have done *anything* to obtain that information."

He winced at the pain in her rapidly rising voice. The pain he had put there. "Josie, you need to listen to me. It wasn't like that."

"Wasn't it?" she asked, turning away from him. "Wasn't it?"

"No!" he insisted. "It wasn't."

"Then how was it?" She looked at him again, but the guard she had finally dropped with him over the past few weeks was back up. "Explain to me, Evan."

He drew a deep breath. "Josie, when you came back to the village, I admit I was perhaps less than thrilled. After all, you hated me. And your presence was always a reminder of the worst of myself."

She folded her arms and said nothing. So he continued.

"When I saw you at my sister's wedding, I was taken aback by you. Genuinely attracted to you." She snorted derision and he scowled. "Please do not deny what I'm saying. It's the truth."

"But?" she encouraged, her tone cold. "Because there is obviously a *but* to all this poetry or else I wouldn't have found you snooping through my things."

"That same afternoon, I realized you might know something about Claire," he admitted. "I spoke to Gabriel about it and he pushed me to pursue that truth."

Her bottom lip trembled, but her voice was strong as she said, "Why you?"

He hesitated. "I'm going to tell you the whole truth, Josie. Even though it may hurt you, but I want you to understand, to see—"

"Why *you*, Evan?" she repeated, folding her arms in that shield once again.

He dropped his gaze from hers. He didn't want to look in her eyes when he said the next words destined to fall from his lips. "Because...because Gabriel believed you might *like* me."

She barked out a pained laugh and moved to the chair

beside her fire. She collapsed into it and stared silently into the flames for a long time. He wanted so badly to speak, but her expression was a warning to him to wait. To let her guide what would happen next.

After all, she had been a victim of everything that had transpired before.

"So you and your brother concocted a plan to take advantage of whatever feelings you thought I had for you," she finally said, her voice rough and almost foreign. "Did you laugh while you did it?"

He moved toward her, guarded as he took the chair next to hers. Her hand was close, but he didn't take it even though he wanted to. Instead he fisted his fingers against the chair arm and said, "Never. I was never comfortable with the idea, Josie. I swear to you that is true. But Gabriel is so desperate to find any information about Claire. He is certain if he could just find her, he could fix this, save her. And his desperation drove me. Just as thoughts of what my sister might be enduring drove me."

Her lips pinched, but he could see his words had somehow hit their mark. She shook her head. "I can't imagine what your loss must be like. Actually, I can, for it is much like mine. But that you would go so far, Evan, that you would woo me, seduce me into giving you information?"

"That wasn't it," he said. "I swear to you it wasn't. The more time I spent with you, the more I wanted you. *You*. That had nothing to do with Claire or Gabriel or anyone else. Everything that transpired between us was the truth, Josie."

She took a long breath and turned her face toward his. Her expression was so pained that it made his own chest hurt. Once more the power of what he had done was evident.

"You can say that all you want, Evan," she whispered. "But your actions tell me that it's a lie. You took me, you pleasured me and you waited until I was asleep to snoop through my things."

"I didn't come here intending to do it. I told Gabriel I

wouldn't," he insisted.

Her face drained of what color remained and she stood up slowly, staring down at him with renewed upset and anger. "That was what Gabriel meant."

He wrinkled his brow in confusion. "What?"

"At the party celebrating our marriage," she explained. "He was drunk and I approached him, hoping to offer some comfort after you told me you two had argued. I wanted to make peace for you."

Of course she would do such a thing, try to be a balm on the trouble between them. That was an utterly Josie thing to do, one of the main things that had drawn him to her despite any connection she might have to Claire.

"What did my brother say?" he asked.

"He said *I* was what you two argued about. Because you wouldn't do what he wanted." Her voice caught with hurt. "He was babbling and I had no idea what he could possibly mean at the time. But now it's so clear. He wanted you to continue to use our connection to leverage information about your sister."

He jumped up. "And he told you I refused, Josie. So that must mean something to you, doesn't it?"

She stared at him, holding his gaze until her scrutiny made him shift with discomfort.

"It might," she finally said. "Except that I found you doing his bidding not five minutes ago. In the end, using me was just as easy for you as it was for him."

He couldn't let that stand. Not now. He reached out to catch her upper arms and drew her closer. She didn't struggle, though her eyes went wide.

"Listen to me, Josie, please, please listen. I didn't seduce you or wed you in order to use you. I care for you. Truly care."

Somehow he expected that confession to soften her. That she would hear him and understand. But her face twisted with more hurt and anger, and she struggled from his grip to back away from him.

"Don't toss me your bones, Evan," she snapped. "Don't

think that just because you have found me pathetic enough to trick that I will continue to dance to your tune."

He drew back in horror. "That isn't what I'm doing. I just want you to see—"

"I see!" she shouted, her anger finally bubbling over as a tear slid down her cheek. "I see perfectly clearly, I assure you. And a part of me even understands. The loss of Claire is so painful and so horrifying and so deep, that perhaps if I thought I might have a chance to find her, I would also betray someone who was in lov—"

She cut herself off with a painful gasp, but Evan knew the word she was going to say. Even the truncated version hit him like a shot to the chest. In love with him? Did Josie truly love him? He had never asked for that, never expected it. If someone had asked him a month ago if he wanted it, he would have said no.

But today his answer felt very different.

"Please, Josie," he whispered. "I wasn't trying to betray you."

"But you have," she said softly. "Because now that I know what your intentions were at the beginning, now that I've seen you were willing to follow through with them even after everything we've shared…well, it poisons everything, doesn't it?"

"No," he said, and his voice was close to a wail. "It doesn't have to."

"It does," she said, and another tear fell. She swiped it away angrily and straightened her spine. "You have come this far, Evan. You have done this much, so I suppose you have earned the truth you sought. Though once you hear it, I doubt it will give you any chance of finding Claire. So all your lies and sacrifices will have been for nothing."

He blinked. "You'll tell me?"

She nodded. "I never thought I was keeping it from you. And though I hesitated to betray confidences, it seems you are determined to rip them from me. So here is the truth. Claire has written to me just four times since her departure with Jonathon Aston. Mostly they are letters very much like she wrote before she left, and their light and airy style cut me to the bone since I know she suffers. She never speaks about her whereabouts and she only vaguely references any unhappiness she feels at her circumstances."

Evan sagged with disappointment. "That is all?"

"No," she said softly. "The very first time she wrote me, she said she knew I must wonder why she left. She told me that she no longer belonged in your family. That she was more like Aston than any Woodley."

He staggered back. "Why, why would she say that?"

"I don't know," she admitted. "After all, I never have an address to respond, do I? So I couldn't prod her. She asked me not to tell your family her feelings. She didn't want to hurt you." She shook her head. "And neither did I. *That* is the secret you sensed me keeping, Evan. A riddle about not belonging that brings you no closer to the truth about why she left or where she is or if you could ever convince her to come home. So you have sacrificed yourself for nothing."

CHAPTER NINETEEN

Evan watched as Josie paced away from him, far away this time, to the other side of the bed they had shared, like she wanted as much space between them as possible. She let out a long sigh.

"Since I'm certain you don't believe me," she continued. "I will very gladly send all of Claire's letters to you once I return to London. You can read them yourself, as you wanted to tonight. I would ask for them back, though. They're precious to me. The letter in my desk in the other room contains no valuable information, though you may take it when you leave."

He blinked, all thoughts of Claire and what this new information meant fleeing in the face of his wife's cold demeanor.

"Leave?" he repeated.

She nodded, motioning to the door behind him. "Yes. I would like for you to go now."

He sucked in his breath. "Josie, you cannot mean that."

She swallowed hard and he saw her fighting her pain, her pride, whatever feelings she still had for him.

"But I do," she finally said.

"No, *no!*" he said, striding across the room, around the bed where she stood. She staggered back into the corner, as if she feared his touch.

"Get out, Evan," she repeated, but the tremor in her voice betrayed her.

"No," he repeated. "I won't."

She made a low sound of frustration in her throat and lunged past him over the bed. "Then I will," she declared, searching around the ground for her nightgown. She caught it up and struggled to detangle it.

While she was distracted, he moved to where she stood yet again, but this time he didn't stop himself from catching her arm and pulling her in. She molded against him, her eyes wild as she stared up at him.

"Don't," he whispered. "Please."

He dropped his lips to hers, his kiss gentle and filled with all the pleading and apologies he could give her. And for a moment, she relaxed into him, her mouth opening, her body receiving. His arms came around her, holding her to him, as he prayed he could make her see how much she meant to him. Prayed he could repair what he had damaged.

As quickly as she had allowed herself to surrender, she pulled away. Her breath was short and filled with pain. Her eyes wide and wild with the same. Even her desire didn't trump it.

"Please go, Evan," she repeated, and the sob that followed her words tore at him more than a blade could have.

He stared at her, her head bent in defeat and humiliation, her shoulders shaking. He had to do what she wanted. Even though it hurt him, even though he didn't want to walk away, right now she needed space from him.

In truth, she had earned it.

"All right," he said softly. "All right, I'll go." She darted her gaze up in question, but didn't respond. He grabbed his shirt, his boots, and moved for the door. There he stopped. "Josie, the only thing I want you to know right now is how sorry I am. I'm sorry, Josie."

He waited for a moment for her response, but again she remained silent. So finally he stepped from the room and left her to her own feelings.

He shut the door behind himself and leaned against it, his

heart throbbing and his head spinning. When he had started this game with Josie, he never thought it would lead to this. Not just this confrontation, but their passion, their connection, their marriage.

He'd never thought he'd destroy it all.

But now he had to think of Josie, as he hadn't before. What did she need? Because giving her that was the only way he might ever get her back.

Evan stood in the foyer of his mother's home less than half an hour later, looking up the stairs. He was waiting, and after the emotional moments of that night, he was having a hard time with patience.

Finally, the person he had been waiting for came running down the stairs.

"What is it?" Josie's mother asked as she tied her dressing gown around her tightly.

He pursed his lips as he moved toward her. "Your daughter is physically fine," he reassured her, and caught her elbow as she sagged with relief. "But she needs you."

Mrs. Westfall gathered her composure and looked at him with question. "I have no idea what you are talking about. Tonight is your wedding night—why in the world would you be here demanding I come down to see you? And why would Josie need me?"

He swallowed hard, hating himself more and more with every passing moment. "I made a promise to you to take care of her. I made the same promise to her," he said slowly. "And I broke it. Stupidly. Selfishly."

Mrs. Westfall drew back. "What did you do?"

"Just go to her. I've had the carriage prepared. Go to her. She needs you now."

Josie's mother shot him a look of disbelief, mistrust and

he turned his face away from it. It was too much like Josie's expression when she caught him going through her things.

But she said nothing else. She merely rushed out the door and left him to watch her ride away, back to her daughter. Back to Josie. Back to the woman who never wanted to see him again.

The woman he wanted more than anything.

Josie sat staring at the dying fire. She had no idea how long she had been sitting there. An hour? Two? A day? It didn't really matter. Everything she had thought she had was gone now. Destroyed with one swift revelation of a lie.

She bent her head and fought the tears that had been threatening since the moment Evan walked out her door and left her to her own thoughts and pains and humiliations.

There was a light knock at her chamber door, and she tensed. "Please, I already asked you to go away, Evan," she called out.

The door opened regardless and she glared up, but was surprised to find it was not her husband but her mother who invaded her privacy and her pain.

"Mama?" she murmured as she rose her feet. "What are you doing here? You were staying at the Woodley estate tonight."

Mrs. Westfall stepped into the chamber and shut the door behind her. Josie could feel her mother's questions, her hesitations and her pity as she looked her up and down.

"Evan came home and fetched me. He said you needed me."

Josie bent her head. "Then you know what happened."

Mrs. Westfall shook her head as she crossed the room and sat down beside her daughter. Then her mother's arms came around her and she held her close.

"I know you need me. If you want to tell me why, I hope you will. If you just want to cry, that is perfectly acceptable too."

Josie drew in a sharp breath and then her body made her choice for her. She sobbed into her mother's shoulder, crying out all the high emotions of the day, of the weeks before, of the feelings she had finally allowed herself to feel, of the disappointment at having her dreams shattered.

And when she had no tears left, she drew back and took the handkerchief her mother offered from somewhere, despite the fact she was in her nightclothes.

Josie laughed weakly as she stared at her. "So you got into a carriage in your nightshift and dressing gown?"

Mrs. Westfall smiled. "He said you needed me, darling. Why would I waste a moment putting on a gown?" She touched Josie's face. "Now, do you want to tell me?"

Josie shook her head. She didn't want to tell *anyone* about this humiliation. How could she say that her new husband didn't want her, had never wanted her, but had gotten too caught up in a ruse meant to obtain information? The world would laugh that she had ever believed his desire for her was real.

"Love, perhaps it would help to say the words," Mrs. Westfall encouraged.

Josie sighed. That wasn't true. But if she wanted to be understood, she didn't have much choice.

"It all started at Audrey's wedding," she began.

For the next half an hour, she talked. The most sordid of the details, when she had to tell her mother about the affair, was difficult. But she had to be honest. Totally honest. By the time she sank back against her chair, her mother was pale, regardless.

"And so he left and apparently fetched you, and here we are," she finished.

"Indeed, here we are," Mrs. Westfall said with a shake of her head. "Josie, I am...I am speechless. Here you were, engaged in such things and I was completely blind to it."

Josie shrugged. "I suppose I wasn't exactly telling the world. And if it had only been our affair, then this would be easier."

"How?" her mother burst out as she leapt to her feet. "At least now you have the protection of the Woodley name."

"What protection? Oh, yes, I suppose if there is a child resulting from tonight or last week then I won't be shamed. But it is more likely than not that there will not be one. And so I am left married to a man who used my attraction to him in order to obtain information."

Mrs. Westfall bent her head. "I can imagine that was rather hard to hear."

"Hard?" Josie dug her nails into her palms. "Humiliating. Heartbreaking. Not hard. Oh, why did I ever believe he wanted me? Why didn't I see that everything he said and did was a lie?"

Mrs. Westfall shifted with discomfort as she retook her seat. She reached out a hand and cupped her daughter's cheek gently. "Are you certain it was?"

Josie tilted her head with an incredulous look. "You think there was any truth to it after what I told you?"

"Josie, you have been mistreated over the years and it makes you doubt those around you," her mother said softly. "But you cannot be blind to this, to him. I saw Evan when he came back to his mother's home tonight. His eyes were filled with regret, with pain. If he didn't care about you at all, why would he fetch me to offer you comfort?"

Josie clenched her teeth. She didn't want to hear about Evan's good qualities at present. She didn't want to picture him taking care of her, thinking of her. The throb of his betrayal was still too strong.

"Evan isn't the worst person," she admitted. "I'm sure he feels terrible that his ruse was revealed."

Her mother pressed her lips together. "And let us talk of his ruse. Why would he take it so far if seducing you was only to find out what you knew about Claire? You were so reluctant to marry and no one else knew what you'd done. He could have walked away the moment it was clear you were not breeding."

"Please don't defend him because you are happy I've finally landed a man." Now it was Josie who stood and walked away.

Mrs. Westfall let out a long sigh. "That isn't my motivation. And I am not defending him in the slightest. Evan will have to answer for what he did, how he misled you. To you and to me. But I'm trying to make you see that everything he said might not be the lie you think it is, darling."

"What could possibly be the truth?" Josie whispered, wishing her eyes didn't fill with tears when she asked the question.

"The way he looked at you today when you wed, that was the truth," her mother said, rising from her place. "The pain on his face when he fetched me, *that* is the truth."

Josie flinched away from the words she didn't want to hear. They gave her hope and that was far too dangerous a feeling in this moment. She couldn't dare to hope there was something left between her and Evan.

Because it wouldn't be enough for him to think well of her or want to make it right and be chums. Not anymore.

But her mother didn't know her thoughts, and continued, "You were there during the development of this relationship, so you know you saw some things that were the truth. Once you face him again—"

Josie spun on her. "Oh, no, please! Please don't make me face him again."

Mrs. Westfall blinked in obvious confusion. "What do you mean?"

"I mean don't make me face him again," Josie repeated. "I don't want to see him or talk to him. I can't look at him!"

Oh God, to look at him now. To see that he didn't love her when she loved him, to know he had merely used her to his ends.

"Dearest," Mrs. Westfall said slowly, approaching her with the same caution that was in her tone. "You are upset and with every right to feel that way. But you must see that you can't walk away or never see him again."

"Why?" Her voice broke on the question.

"Because you are married. And you did nothing wrong. But if you hide, it will seem like you did. And *they* will talk."

"And you care that I don't ruin our family's reputation any more than I have over the years I was a spinster?" Josie asked.

"No." Her mother touched her cheek. "I care because I know *you* care. If you slink away, you won't be able to show your face again. But if you hold your head up high—"

Josie pictured having to walk into a ballroom with the world staring at her, and her stomach turned. "I can't. Please let me go to the country—"

Her mother shook her head. "You are *in* the country, Jocelyn. This trouble started in the country."

"You know what I mean," Josie pleaded. "Let me go somewhere secluded and just…just pretend it never happened. Don't make me see him right now. Don't make me face him while he tries to explain to me how and why he did this."

Mrs. Westfall squeezed her eyes shut, and for a long time she seemed to be considering Josie's request. Then she frowned. "Sequestering yourself in the country is not the right decision."

Josie's heart sank. "Mama!"

"*But*," her mother continued, "I can understand why you would want to leave here right now. Why staying would be painful. So we will return to London tomorrow."

Josie bent her head. *London.* It was not her favorite place, but it was better than Idleridge at present. At least she would have space from Evan.

"All right," she agreed softly. "I will take London, as long as it's not here." She glanced up to find her mother looking at her with an expression that cut her to her very core. "Oh,

Mama, please don't pity me. I cannot take it."

Mrs. Westfall flew to her. "I feel no pity, darling, none at all. What I feel is heartbroken that you are hurt. What I feel is that you deserved better than this. And I wish I could take away your pain."

With that her mother folded her into her arms and held her as the tears Josie had been fighting fell once more. Fell for herself, fell for the loss of what she thought she had been building with Evan and fell for the future she now realized was never a reality.

CHAPTER TWENTY

As Edward strode into the breakfast room the next morning, Evan looked up from the paper he hadn't even been pretending to read. His older brother screeched to a stop midway to the coffee on the side bar and stared at him.

"What are you doing here?" he asked. "You and Josie were spending the night at her family home, weren't you? I didn't think we'd see you for days."

Evan pursed his lips, trying to mask the pain that ripped through his entire body at his brother's quip. "Josie asked me to leave."

His brother's jaw dropped, and for what seemed like an eternity, he didn't speak. Then he took a place at the table to Evan's left and said, "Tell me everything."

Evan stared at Edward. Right now he desperately needed a confidante, but Gabriel was sleeping off a hangover and, in truth, Evan didn't want to talk to his partner in deception about what their plan had wrought.

He and Edward hadn't been as close as they once were lately, but as he searched his brother's face, he knew Edward would be fair, he would be there.

"When Josie first returned to the shire, it became clear that she and Claire had been communicating. So Gabriel and I came up with a plan to find out what she knew."

Edward blinked. "You think Claire and Josie are writing to each other?"

"Well, Claire writes to Josie, at any rate," he muttered, thinking of that letter in his sister's hand, thinking of Josie's face as she caught him reading it.

Edward frowned. "I suppose it isn't a surprise to hear that. They are best friends. But what kind of plan could you and Gabriel have possibly concocted?"

"Gabriel believed Josie might be the key in finding our sister, so we thought perhaps I could...I could...*trade* on certain attractions between us."

His brother went very still. "But Josie hated you."

"It turns out she did not," he said softly. "And I used her deeper feelings to grow closer to her in the hopes that she would tell me what she knew. And when she didn't and when our attraction got a bit out of control, I-I married her. But last night, she caught me going through her letters and the truth came out. So she asked me to go, and that is why I'm here."

Edward pushed his chair back with a screech, his face twisted in horror. "What the hell are you talking about?" he asked. "What the hell were you thinking?"

"I don't know," Evan admitted, banging his forehead down on the edge of the table. "She was here, and Gabriel was talking about Claire and the line between flirtation and seduction, and I spent time with her, and then it was out of control."

"You listened to bloody *Gabriel*?" Edward snapped. "He is the most intelligent person I know, but when it comes to Claire, he has a blind spot the size of a sailboat."

"He thought Josie might be the key to finding her," Evan repeated as he looked at Edward again. His brother's face was red with anger and he was waving his hands around.

"Gabriel thinks *everything* might be the key to finding Claire!" Edward shouted. "Fuck, if there was a tiny sliver of hope he would interrogate trees and goddamn flowers!"

Evan shook his head. "Yes, I suppose that is true."

"God, you are an idiot. You lied and manipulated yourself into a marriage, Evan," Edward continued, pacing the room relentlessly. "That is permanent."

"I realize that," Evan grumbled.

"And you did it for some tiny shred of thought that Josie might lead us to Claire?" Edward snorted out a sound of derision. "Oh, and poor Josie! If she kicked you out after discovering the truth in your reasons for pursuit, that implies she must have thought you actually *cared* about her."

Evan jumped to his own feet. "I did!" he snapped out. Then he hung his head. "I-I do."

Edward stopped waving his arms and just stared at Evan, blinking. "Oh. Oh, I see."

"Don't *I see* me."

"I just…it isn't expected, that's all." Edward shook his head.

"Why?" Evan asked, moving toward his brother. "You didn't know I deceived Josie, so why did you *think* I married her?"

"Honestly?" Edward shifted with discomfort. "I-I thought you were being forced to."

Evan wrinkled his brow. "Why?"

"Well, it is no secret that you and Josie have never gotten along. I saw at Audrey's wedding that perhaps there was a reluctant attraction there. When we received word you were to marry her, I thought maybe you had behaved imprudently. I assumed I would hear the whole truth eventually, but this?"

Evan gritted his teeth. "First off, Josie is a beautiful woman. It should surprise no one that she should be desired or that a man would want to woo her or wed her."

Edward blinked. "I never said otherwise, Evan. Calm yourself. There is no need to clench that fist." He motioned to the hand Evan didn't even know he had gripped. "Why don't you just explain yourself to me? You are practically bubbling with emotion, so release some of it."

"I did listen to Gabriel," he said slowly. "And I did start out my pursuit of Josie with ulterior motives. But it got…complicated."

He shook his head as he thought of the day they had spent together visiting the tenants, the time they had spent giving each other pleasure, but also coming to know each other.

"Things often do with women we care for," Edward mused, drawing Evan from his thoughts.

"Yes, you are correct that there is an element of force to the marriage," Evan continued. "I allowed things to go too far, but not out of manipulation. I wanted Josie. I needed her. And I think perhaps some part of me knew that if I went too far, I would be given a reason to marry her. I wanted it, Edward. I wanted her to be my wife."

Edward nodded slowly. "I see."

"And I intended to tell her the truth about why I started my pursuit." Evan sighed. "Josie is uncertain about herself, about us, about me, and I thought if I just waited a little while, let her feel how good we were together, that the truth would have less sting."

Edward tilted his head and looked at Evan with eyes that saw too much. "But then you say she caught you going through your things, so why did you do that?"

"Oh God, I don't know. Gabriel was telling me I didn't care for Claire and it rang in my ears. Josie fell asleep after— well, after—and I was in her chamber. I kept hearing Gabriel's voice saying this was my only chance, saying I didn't care enough to sacrifice, to do the hard things. I kept thinking of Claire suffering, maybe even dying, if I didn't help her. I thought if I just looked it would close the topic. I didn't think Josie would find me. I didn't think I would ruin everything."

Edward nodded like he understood, and in a way, Evan supposed he did. After all, his older brother had suffered greatly in his first marriage, and his second to Mary had not come on the smoothest of paths.

"And when the truth came out, did you also tell Josie that you love her?" his brother asked softly.

The question rolled over Evan like a wave, knocking him backward a few steps. "Love. I-I never said love. I care for

Josie, yes. I want her, of course. But love her?"

Only the words didn't seem as foreign or false as he thought they would. Love Josie. *Was* this love?

Before he could talk to his brother more about it, there was a knock on the breakfast room door and their mother's butler appeared. "I am sorry to disturb, my lords, but Mrs. Westfall is here to talk to Lord Evan."

Evan bolted toward the door. "Please, I want to see her."

The butler stepped aside and revealed Mrs. Westfall as she approached the room. As he bowed away, Evan stared at his new mother-in-law. She was glaring at him.

"How is Josie?" he whispered.

"As poorly as can be expected," was her snapped reply. She looked past him toward Edward. "My lord. I assume your wastrel of a brother has crowed to you about his misdeeds?"

Edward bowed his head. "I know what he has done, though I promise you, he was not crowing."

"No?" Mrs. Westfall said, her attention returning to Evan. "I hope that is true."

Evan took a step toward her. "I take *no* pleasure in your daughter's pain."

Her eyebrows lifted. "That may be true, but you still caused it."

"I did. And I hate myself."

"Good." Mrs. Westfall nodded. "Good. Then perhaps there is some hope. Josie does not know I am here. But I thought you should know that my daughter and I are leaving within the hour."

Evan drew back. "Leaving! What? Where? Why?"

Mrs. Westfall observed him closely and took a moment to answer. "Yes. Josie has insisted she wants to go. It took a great deal of negotiating to get her to agree to return to London, which answers the question of where. You already know why, don't you?"

"Yes," Evan whispered, his tone broken. "But I must speak to her."

"I happen to agree, but right now is not the optimal time, I don't think." Mrs. Westfall clenched her hands at her sides as if thinking about this subject hurt her. "Josie's pain would not allow her to hear anything you had to say to her right now."

Evan cleared his throat, wishing he could erase the lump there. "What should I do?"

"Wait a few days, I think. Allow her to have some space to think about what has happened. And to miss you, which I think she already does."

"I miss her too," Evan admitted.

Her eyes narrowed with disbelief, but she didn't voice it as she said, "Then you come to her when she's had a bit of time. If you care for my daughter, you had best be ready and willing to fight. But if you don't…" Mrs. Westfall trailed off and caught her breath, as if the very idea hurt her. "Well, if you don't, then I hope you will be honest for once. Don't bob her around on your string while you whisper empty platitudes."

Evan dipped his head. He deserved this woman's disgust. He deserved Josie's as well. And though the idea of waiting, of letting Josie leave him and just praying he could catch her, chafed, he knew Mrs. Westfall was right. He had to do what was best for Josie right now, not himself.

"I will follow in three days," he vowed. "And I will fix this."

Mrs. Westfall looked him up and down, her contempt plain on her face. "I certainly hope you can, sir. For her sake."

Then she nodded to his brother and left the room without another word. As soon as she was gone, Evan buckled into the closest chair and set his head in his hands.

"I did this," he whispered, hating himself.

Edward came to stand beside him and reached down to squeeze his shoulder. "You did. But now you have some time to decide."

"Decide what?" Evan asked, lifting his head to look at his brother. He saw Edward's pity.

"Decide if you're going to admit you love this girl and

fight for her until the bitter end, or if you're going to let her go and find some way to atone for the damage you've done to you both. Only you can decide that, Evan. Only *you* can know what you're willing to do."

"What I'm willing to do," Evan repeated as his mind went once again to Josie and all they had shared. He'd been trying to avoid loving her, fearing that emotion. Fearing it with her. But now that he was a hair's breath away from losing her, he could deny it no longer. "I am willing to do everything, anything to win her back," he vowed. "Because I love her."

"Good." His brother smiled. "Then you have three days to plan all the ways you are going to woo her."

CHAPTER TWENTY-ONE

Josie glared at the new bouquet of flowers her maid had just deposited in her chamber. They rested next to four others that had been delivered over the past few days.

"Frustrating man," she muttered as she leaned in to smell the intoxicating mixture of lilac and roses. "Why must he woo me?"

The first three days since her return to London had been uneventful. She had been left alone, even her mother hadn't pushed her too hard. She'd lain in her bed, staring out the window, and been allowed to wallow in her feelings.

But then Evan had begun his attentions. He was obviously back in London and had made his presence known through unopened letters that sat on her bedside table, visits she had refused and flowers, flowers, flowers. All her favorite flowers.

"Why can't he just let me go?" she whispered to herself as she flopped down on her bed. "Why does his honor drive him to make this right when it can never be right?"

Of course, that was a difficult attitude to keep when he was trying so desperately. Sometimes she wondered if she was just being petulant, turning away out of hurt and not willing to hear him.

But then she thought of the guilt on his face when she caught him reading her letters. Of the realization that he had been playing her for a fool all along, and her resolve stiffened again.

She would not see him. Because seeing him would be too cruel. Of course, that meant locking out everyone else in is world too. Audrey had also called during the past few days, as had Mary, but she had turned them away as well. She wanted no champions of Evan to confuse her. Or pity her.

She threw an arm over her face and let out a muffled grumble.

"Great Lord, Josie, you cannot lay about in bed all day!"

She moved her arm and looked up to see her mother standing in the doorway. The same look of concern that had been on her face since she learned of Josie's troubles lined her features now.

Josie sat up. "I wasn't lying in bed. I was lying *on* the bed, and there is a distinction."

Mrs. Westfall's eyes narrowed slightly. "Only the tiniest distinction, my dear. But regardless, it is time to get ready."

Josie pushed to her feet and folded her arms. "Mama, I have already told you three times today that I will not go to the Duke and Duchess of Hartholm's ball!"

"Yes, you have told me three times," her mother agreed, even as she strolled past Josie to her wardrobe and opened it wide. She flicked through the dozens of pretty dresses inside as she continued speaking. "But I still don't understand why."

"Don't you?" Josie huffed. "Mama, the Duke of Hartholm is the brother to Crispin Flynn. Who attended my wedding with his wife Gemma. Who is the sister of Mary, who is the wife of Edward, who is Evan's brother."

Mrs. Westfall leaned away from the wardrobe for a moment and shook her head. "That is rather like all the begetting in the Bible. So many connections."

"Please do not obtain a sense of humor now," Josie said as she folded her arms.

"I've always had a sense of humor, darling," Her mother said with a light laugh. She pulled Josie's favorite gown from the closet, a pale green silk that fell in the most flattering way and brought out her eyes. "I will send in Nell and you should get dressed. We have less than an hour before we are to depart."

"No," Josie said, sitting down on the edge of her bed with a scowl. "I have told you I will not."

Mrs. Westfall turned on her and there was no frustration or anger on her face, even as she said, "My love, you are an adult and a married lady. Under normal circumstances, I would not be able to force you to do anything you did not want to do. I would respect your wishes. But since you have chosen to return to my home, I'm afraid I will continue to make decisions that are best for you."

"How in the world is going to the Hartholm ball *best* for me?" Josie demanded.

Her mother shrugged. "You have been holed up in this house since your return to London and people are beginning to talk."

Josie froze, for the thought of their whispers grated along her spine. "And why would I want to face that?"

"Because you have done nothing wrong. I want you to hold your head up high and show the world that you are above that foolishness. The Flynn family—which is where the Hartholms originate, of course—for all their popularity now, experienced their own set of scandals and have overcome them for the most part. What better place to raise your chin and show the world how strong you are?"

"And what if I am not strong?" Josie asked. "What if Evan is there?"

Mrs. Westfall's gaze flitted away. "He is likely not invited. Right now I do not think that Evan is a favorite amongst his family, thanks to his actions toward you."

"So they all know?" Josie asked dully.

"You must have known that they would find out. You can't just run off the day after your wedding without a family noticing." Her mother inclined her head slightly.

"There's that sense of humor again," Josie muttered. "But I suppose you are correct. Can I not convince you to let me bow out of this ball? Perhaps allow me to run off to that secluded countryside hideaway I have been begging for?"

"You cannot." Her mother grasped her hand and squeezed. "The longer you avoid this, the worse it will be."

Josie shook her head. "Fine. Send in Nell. I won't fight her."

"Good," her mother said, her eyes brightening as she left the room.

But as Josie walked to the bed where her ball gown lay, she flinched. The very idea of facing off with not just Society but also the family of her now-estranged husband was not in any way pleasant. And all she could hope to do was survive it and not have much attention called to herself.

As the Duke and Duchess of Hartholm's ball went on around them, Evan cast a glance at Audrey and Jude, but his sister only glared at him in return. He folded his arms.

"You and I arrived back in London the same day," he said, sidling up to her so his words would not be too loud and be overheard by the crush of the crowd. "And in those four days, I think you have spoken to me three times. And two of those were to call me an idiot."

Audrey tilted her head. "You *are* an idiot, Evan. An idiot. There, now I have spoken to you four times in four days and called you an idiot every time."

Evan shifted and looked to his new brother-in-law and longtime friend for assistance, but Jude offered none. "Don't expect me to take your side, Evan. I like my wife and don't want her to kick me out of her bed."

Audrey shot Jude a look. "And?"

"Oh, and I also think you're an idiot," Jude added. He leaned forward. "I actually do. It isn't just for my wife's sake."

"Well, I am not arguing that what I did was wrong," Evan

growled. "Everyone telling me over and over doesn't help. I'm trying to fix it, but Josie won't allow me to do so. I call on her every day—*twice* a damn day."

Audrey's hard expression softened a fraction. "I've heard from her mother that Josie will be here tonight. So you have been given every opportunity thanks to our friends the Flynns and your mother-in-law. You will have to take advantage."

Evan's heart lurched to his throat. He hadn't seen Josie in a week. Now he ached for just a glimpse of his wife. But the fact was that he had no idea if she would let him near her at all, let alone allow him to speak to her in private so he could begin to repair the damage he had done.

"When will she arrive?" he asked, peering over the crowd, impatience burning inside of him.

"Calm yourself," came Edward's voice from behind him.

Evan turned to frown as his brother and Mary approached. Mary and Audrey exchanged hugs and Jude and Edward shook hands, but soon all their attention was back on him.

"She has not yet arrived?" Mary pressed, the most gentle in her approach of all his judgmental family.

And yet he could not take solace in her kindness, for he knew he didn't deserve it. In fact, he deserved far worse than his brother and sister's pointed judgment as well.

"No," he said, looking over the crowd with impatience a second time. "Perhaps she changed her mind."

He wouldn't put it past her. After all, Josie knew he was in Town, thanks to his multiple attempts to see her. She would be a fool not to guess that he might be in attendance at this ball, since the Flynn family was so connected to his own.

But he had no sooner had that troubling thought when the footman at the door intoned, "Mrs. Westfall and Lady Evan Hartwell."

Around them the crowd stirred and many heads swiveled to watch as Josie and her mother made their entrance. Evan could hardly breathe as he got his first glimpse of her in what felt like a lifetime.

She was glorious. There was no other word for it. Her pale green gown flowed over her lush body, demure and yet still hinting at the wonderful curves he adored. Her hair had been fixed and twisted and curled into an elaborate homage to Ancient Greece. Little tendrils framed her face. And though he was too far across the room to see her green eyes, he knew the color she wore would complement them perfectly and bring out their brightness and vitality.

Mary moved forward. "I will go to her first, Evan. Wait here."

He didn't answer. He couldn't. He was too mesmerized by watching Josie—his wife—enter the room. Her gaze swept around her and he knew she was searching for him. From her frown, it seemed that was not a happy thing.

He lunged to go to her, but Edward caught his arm and held him steady. "Wait now. Let Mary and Gemma introduce her to Serafina and Rafe."

"How can I wait?" he snapped, trying and failing to shake his brother off.

"Allow her to get comfortable at least," Audrey said with a shake of her head. "Run up to her now and you risk sending her flying from the room. Good Lord, you must be in love if you can't even utilize a bit of strategy."

He spun on his sister. "I am not trying to devise the proper strategy to speak to my own wife."

Jude lifted both eyebrows at his sharpness. "Perhaps you should listen to your sister. Audrey knows Josie, after all."

"Not as well as I do," Evan grumbled, turning back to watch as Mary greeted Josie with a warm hug. He was pleased that Josie accepted it and even allowed her mother to slip away from her.

Mary linked arms with Josie and they moved across the floor. People looked at her as they went and Evan could see how she lifted her chin in defiance even in the face of their scrutiny. He found his heart swelling with pride at her strength of character, for he knew their whispers and pointed attention put her to mind of unhappy times.

The two women soon approached the Duchess of Hartholm and Mary's sister Gemma, and it was clear introductions were being made. From the expressions, all the women were trying to make things easier on Josie. How he appreciated that. And he was especially pleased when his wife actually smiled and it seemed...*real.*

"What should I do?" he asked, directing the question to Audrey without looking at her.

Audrey was quiet for a moment as she observed Josie beside him. "She seems more at ease now," his sister said.

"She's looking this way," Evan gasped as Josie's eyes fell on him. She jolted at the sight of him and turned her face, but her cheeks went pink and her posture stiffened.

"Go," Audrey encouraged him with a slight push. "Ask her to dance with you. She will not be able to refuse with the crowd watching. Just try not to make an ass of yourself once you have her in your arms."

He glowered one last time at his sister, but then marched into the crowd toward Josie. It was obvious the women with her noted his approach, and from the way she stiffened more and more, so did she. But she didn't run. And for that he was grateful.

As he reached her, he saw those in the crowd watching, leaning in. Clearly the fact that they were married but already living apart was fodder for gossip.

"Good evening, ladies," he drawled, hoping to sound casual when he could hardly hear over the pounding of his heart.

The others said their hellos, but Josie didn't respond. She just stared straight ahead, as if frozen by her pain. Or her hatred.

"Josie," he said.

She slowly turned. "My lord," she said, her tone icy.

"I have come to ask for a dance, Josie," he said, holding out a hand so those around them could see.

"I don't want to dance," she replied in a low tone.

Mary, Gemma and Serafina all flinched at her refusal and each took a small step back as they pretended to go into deep conversation so as not to intrude upon this private moment any more than they had to.

"People are watching," he said softly. "Take my hand, Josie. Do it this once and I promise you, I will not demand it again."

She stared at his outstretched hand for a very long moment. Then she sighed. "I don't know that your promises can be trusted, but what choice do you give me?"

Then she set her palm in his.

Even through her gloves, the jolt of awareness that touching her gave him was enough to make his knees shake. God, but he wanted to carry her out of this room. He wanted to kiss her until she could no longer deny him. He wanted to hold her until she never wanted to leave.

But in this moment, what *he* wanted didn't matter. This moment was about her.

He guided her forward to the dance floor and they moved into the gathered couples.

"I hope it's a country reel," she murmured under her breath.

But instead the strains of the waltz rose up around them. Evan smiled. Thank God for small favors. He placed a hand on her hip and with the other positioned her hand, and they moved into the steps together.

"This will be easier if you look at me," he said softly after the first few steps.

"I would prefer not to," she said, but she did lift her gaze and found his. He caught his breath at how beautiful she looked.

"I have missed you."

Her lips thinned into a frown. "Don't lie anymore. You have already gotten all the information I have to share. There is no need to make us both into fools."

"I am a fool," he said, holding her gaze even as he maneuvered her. "But you never were."

"I was the worst fool," she whispered, and the way her voice broke cut him to his core.

"I'm so sorry," he said. "Please hear how sincere that is."

"I hear it," she admitted, and for a moment he was lifted by hope. "But I've noted your sincerity before and been so very wrong. How can I do anything but doubt myself and you now?"

He hesitated. "I deserve that, Josie. But won't you let me call on you tomorrow? Won't you let me try to make everything up to you?"

She was silent as the music carried on and they danced around and around. But the song was more than half finished. Their time together was running out.

"Please," he urged.

She slowly shook her head. "I know you won't understand, Evan. You couldn't. But I have spent my life not feeling like I was important. And with you, I thought I was. But then the truth came out and I knew that no matter what you said or did, you would never have wanted me if I hadn't been useful through the information I had. I can't pretend that isn't true. And I can't face the pain again. Especially with you. You who I...who meant something."

The song slowed and then stopped, and the dancers began to leave the floor. Josie stared up at him, her pale face reflecting all the pain he felt, all the pain he'd caused.

"It was never meant to be us," she whispered. "That future was false from the first moment you spoke to me. Later we will work out what happens next. But for now, I can't go back. Back is too painful. You don't have to torture yourself, Evan. But just be happy that you can let go."

"I don't want to let go," he murmured, hardly able to breathe enough to speak with the weight of her leaving on his mind.

"Then I will," she whispered, and turned to go.

He snaked a hand out and caught her wrist gently, refusing to let her walk away.

"Not like this," he said.

CHAPTER TWENTY-TWO

Josie stared at Evan's lean, tanned fingers wrapped around her wrist like a beautiful manacle and she shivered. Why couldn't he just allow her this escape? Why did he have to keep pursuing her? Out of what? Honor? Guilt?

She didn't want that.

"Evan, we've had our dance," Josie said under her breath, trying to keep the smile on her face for the increasingly interested crowd when inside she was screaming. "Our last dance. And I'm going home. So please stop pretending to give a damn." He opened his mouth to speak, but she finally pulled from his grip. "Please."

She turned away and walked from the dance floor. Her hands were shaking, her heart aching, but this was what she had to do.

"Jocelyn, stop!"

She was at least ten feet away when Evan shouted those words. She froze, watching as the rest of the ballroom stirred, looked at her, looked behind her. What was he doing? Was she not humiliated enough?

"Please stop!" he repeated just as loudly. "And look at me."

Her cheeks burned as she faced him in one sweeping turn. "What are you doing?" she asked through clenched teeth.

Women were whispering behind their fans now, men were grinning as they looked at her. It was a nightmare. A horrible memory of her very worst nights in ballrooms just like this. Even worse, it was *Evan* creating this pain.

On purpose. When she had already told him just a short time before that she didn't want this.

"You will not let me declare myself in private," he said as he took a step toward her. "So I have no choice but to say these words before the world. Perhaps it's better that way."

"How can this be better?" Josie said, shaking her head as she prayed for the floor to open up and devour her.

"Because then *everyone* will know the truth, not just you," he said. "Please let me speak."

"You will do what you like, why bother asking for permission?" she snapped as she folded her arms and steeled herself against this further humiliation.

She caught a glimpse of her mother standing along the dance floor edge with Mary and Edward, Audrey and Jude, and Mary's sister Gemma and her husband Crispin Flynn. All of them looked shocked, though her mother's face was twisted in equal horror to her own. Perhaps now that Josie was publicly humiliated, her mother would let her cloister herself in the country for good, at last.

"What was said to you as a girl," he began. "What was done to you by me and by so many in this room...Josie, you deserved better."

Her mouth dropped open. "What?"

"You deserved better than the cruelty of these people, many of whom are not fit to shine your shoe." He moved closer again. "I include myself in that group. That I, whether by accident or not, was any part of your pain is abominable to me."

Josie shifted and her gaze flitted to the crowd. There were a few there who actually looked chagrined at his words. Some still looked cruel and triumphant. Her heart thudded so loudly she could scarcely hear above it.

But Evan continued, "When you came to Idleridge just before Audrey's wedding, I admit I was not honest with you.

And you deserved better then as well."

There was a gasp through the crowd, but now Josie hardly heard it. Evan was staring at her so closely, his dark gaze holding her in place, reminding her of things both sweet and bitter. She could only look at him now, nothing else mattered.

"I am a liar, just as you accused me of being," he continued.

She nodded slowly. "Well, at least you can admit it."

"I can," he said. "And I will add that I am not good enough to be with you, Josie. You are too fine and fair, too smart, too lovely, too kind to lower yourself to me. But we are married now, so you are bound to me despite all my failings."

Josie tilted her head. Were those tears in his eyes? Just a sparkle of them as he stepped one more step closer? They *were*, and her heart all but stopped.

"What are you doing?"

"The biggest lie I ever told wasn't the one I told to you."

She sucked in a breath. "There were more?"

He nodded. "Just one. And I told it to myself," he said. "And it was that I didn't love you."

She staggered slightly, but he caught her elbow and kept her from collapsing in front of half the *ton*.

"My saving grace, perhaps my only one, is that I love you, Josie. I love you with everything that is good in me. And even though I know you deserve better, I can only hope that there is some small part of you that might love me a little bit in return. That might see past the lie I told you on an evening that seems so long ago and see the truth in what I'm telling you now."

She stared at him, unable to speak, unable to form a thought coherent enough to share. What he said was her fantasy, but was it true? Did he mean this declaration of love? Could he possibly?

She looked into his eyes, tried to find the lie, but all she saw was truth.

"Do I have to go to my knees?" he asked softly.

Before she could answer, he did just that, dropping before

her in supplication. "Please," he said.

"Oh God, say yes!" came an unidentified female voice from the crowd.

It shocked Josie into looking around. The room was all but silent, every eye on them. Evan was doing this not to humiliate her, but to atone. To declare himself in a way that was so public it had to be true. He was humiliating *himself*, not her, to put them on some kind of equal ground. Doing it forced her to feel what she had been trying to avoid, forced her to see what she thought was an illusion and forced her to speak to save him.

"I love you," she whispered, then raised her voice so the leaning crowd could hear. "I love you, Evan. And while I hate what set us on this path, there is nowhere else I would rather be than here with you, as your wife."

He stood up in one smooth motion. "Will you come home with me, then?"

She hesitated just a fraction of a second before she nodded. With a yelp of relief and pleasure, he caught her in his arms and then his mouth came down on hers, eliciting yet another gasp from the crowd, followed by a surprising burst of applause.

One Josie hardly heard and for once in her life didn't care about. Because she was with Evan. She was with her husband and the love of her life. The man who broke their kiss, grinned down at her and then promptly tucked her hand into the crook of his arm and guided her from the ballroom without further comment or question.

Evan pulled Josie into his lap as the carriage began to rumble toward his London townhome and wrapped his arms around her, reveling in the warmth of her pressed to him. The pleasure and promise of her.

She gazed up at him, a small but hesitant smile on her face. "I thought we'd talked before about you standing up in front of the world and making defenses."

He smiled as he smoothed his fingers across her cheek. Soft as satin, just as he remembered. "That was a declaration, not a defense," he clarified. "And I had to do it, Josie. I feared you would walk away forever. I had to show you how much you mean to me."

"Enough to humiliate yourself in front of family, friends, acquaintances and strangers," she whispered.

"Well, I don't consider it a humiliation," he said. "I hurt you. And not just once. And I hate myself for that."

"But did you mean what you said? That what started as a lie turned into truth?"

"I meant every word." He stroked a thumb over her full lower lip. "Josie, I did approach you at first with the idea that you could help me find my sister. But with every moment we spent together, I knew that you meant more to me. When I touched you, when I kissed you, as I fell in love with you, that had nothing to do with manipulation."

Her smile grew. "Say that you love me again."

He leaned in and brushed his lips over hers gently. "I love you, Jocelyn. With all my heart."

She wrapped her arms around him. "I love you too. Now show me."

He drew back. "Right here in the carriage?"

She nodded. "Unless you are stronger than I am and can wait until we reach your home."

"No, I am most definitely not strong enough," he whispered before he devoured her mouth once more.

She opened for him willingly and he dove inside, tasting her sweetness, coaxing a moan from deep within her that seem to bind them with pleasure. He reached around as he drew her closer so she straddled his lap, and began to knead her backside through her pretty gown.

"God, you were beautiful tonight," he growled as he

tugged her skirts higher and she shifted so that he could bunch them between them. "But all I could think about was what was under this dress."

He pushed his hand between them and found the slit in her drawers. Sliding inside, he stroked his fingers across her sex and found her wet for him already. She gasped at the touch and her head dropped back.

"I wanted you too, even though I hated myself for it," she panted. "And you for being so irresistible even when I was determined not to let you in."

"Let me in now," he asked as he pressed his index finger to her opening.

"Yes," she moaned as he glided inside her tight channel. "Yes."

He stroked her gently, returning his mouth to hers as he pumped one finger, then two inside her squeezing body. She arched against him, meeting his thrusts with mewling whimpers that turned to cries when he pressed his thumb to her clitoris and took her over the edge of pleasure.

As her body shuddered around his fingers, he slid his opposite hand between them to loosen his trousers, freeing his aching cock. She shifted as his fingers popped from her wet sex and positioned herself over him. He tensed, but she didn't lower her body to his.

Instead she cupped his cheeks. "I love you, Evan."

Four words. Words she had already said, but with their bodies nearly joined and her eyes locked with his, his throat swelled. "I love you, Josie," he whispered back, then pushed upward to slide into her.

She didn't shut her eyes as he filled her, but held his stare. And when she moved, it was the most intense, powerful and passionate thing he had ever experienced. She rose over him in strong, sure thrusts, taking him and releasing him. But she never looked away.

"Come for me, Evan," she whimpered, mimicking what he had said to her so many times in the course of their affair.

And those soft words did for him what they had done for her. The pleasure built and he let out a sharp cry as his seed began to move. At the same time, her pace quickened and her expression lit up with the pleasure they shared. They came together, rocking in time to the carriage as she kissed him once more with all her passion and love.

She collapsed against his chest with a laughing sigh and he put his arms around her to hold her tight.

"I swear to you, wife, at some point we will make love in a bed without any drama or potential interruption."

She glanced up at him and her love shone in her eyes. "Oh, Evan...what fun would that be?"

Then she lifted up and kissed him once more.

EPILOGUE

Three months later

Josie stepped into the dining room to find Evan at his place at the head of the table, the paper in his hand. She smiled in this moment when he had not yet noticed her. They had only been married a short time, but he had filled that time with all the love and promises she could have wanted. Where she had once been uncertain, now she knew...

He loved her as much as she loved him. And the past had no power over them.

"Are you going to stare at me until luncheon is served, or come and give me a kiss?" he asked, looking up from this paper to speak with what she imagined was meant to be a stern glance.

She laughed and all but danced into the dining room. "And shock the servants?"

He smiled as he set the paper away, caught her hand and drew her into his lap. "Our poor servants are already so very scandalized. What is one more kiss to scar them?"

She bent her head and gave him his prize, sinking into the pressure of his lips and surrendering to the pleasure it awoke in her each and every time.

When they finally parted she wrapped her arms around his neck. "I had a letter from your mother this morning."

"Did you?" he asked, even as he stroked her thigh beneath

the table in a most distracting fashion.

"I did," she said, her breath hitching. "She is going to return to London next week. With Gabriel."

Evan's hand stopped stroking and she saw him frown slightly. Although they had both received letters from Gabriel since their departure from Idleridge months before, he had not returned to London with the rest of the family. It would be the first time Josie saw him since their wedding.

"Will you receive my brother?" Evan asked softly.

She smiled. "Of course. Truly, as hurt as I was by how things transpired, I have always understood why. Gabriel and Claire have been close as siblings could be since the moment they were born. He is driven to find her—how could I hate him?"

Evan's face relaxed slightly. "Good. And perhaps we can be of some help to him. I am pleased they will return. Miss Gray must think Mama is quite recovered to let her loose."

"Well, that is the interesting thing," Josie said, rising from her place in her husband's lap and taking a seat beside him instead. "Your mother intends to have Miss Gray join us for the holidays and a short time after."

Evan wrinkled his brow. "She does?"

"Apparently so," Josie said. "And I'm glad. I like Juliet a great deal and I think we could help her find a very fine match of her own."

Evan drew back. "You intend to play matchmaker?"

She nodded. "If she wishes it and if I can be of any help, I would try." She tangled her fingers with his. "After all, I want all my friends to be as happy as I am."

"Happy as us?" Evan whispered, leaning in close to her lips. "Impossible."

Then he kissed her, and she forgot about anything in the world but him.

Look for the next chapter in The Wicked Woodleys series with Tempted, featuring the youngest brother Gabriel, coming January 2016.

Excerpt of Tempted
THE WICKED WOODLEYS BOOK 3

In her role as healer, Juliet Gray had been to the palatial estate on the hill dozens and dozens of times in the past four months, but every time the gates opened and she saw it rising above her, her heart fluttered wildly. At first it had been from nervousness that she would not be able to help the mistress of this house through an illness. Lady Woodley had been very sick when Juliet first arrived and having lost a mother herself, she had perfectly understood the grave faces of the adult children of the Dowager Marchioness.

Later, when the lady was out of danger and only needing support as she recovered, Juliet's discomfort had come from a feeling of not belonging in the grand house. Until she had been called upon by the wife of the current Marquis to help, Juliet had never served anyone in the titled class. She didn't know if she was supposed to talk to the lady and her children or try to disappear into the wallpaper so as not to bother them with her commonness. But she had found the entire family to be warm and welcoming, none more than Lady Woodley, herself, so soon that twinge of fear had faded.

But it had been replaced with another anxiety. One that she scarcely wished to name, even in her own head. One that had to do with Lady Woodley's third son, Gabriel. Lord Gabriel, if she was to be technical about it, which she always strove to be since she feared if she were too forward, even in the safety of her own mind, that she would show too much to the world at large.

Would he be there today? Waiting up in that house with his stern expressions and occasionally furtive glances? With his pointed questions and unexpected...

No, she mustn't think about that.

"You are very pale," her father said, interrupting her thoughts as their modest carriage came to a stop in the round driveway. They would have exactly twenty seconds now before the door was opened by the servants. Juliet knew them well, after all her visits here.

She forced a smile for her father. "Am I? And what of you? You look nervous as a schoolboy seeing a girl for the first time!"

He chuckled and her heart warmed at the sound. "I suppose it isn't very often that I am invited the home of a Dowager Marchioness, is it? I have certainly never accompanied you here before."

Juliet somehow maintained her smile, but inside her father's words echoed her own discomfort. Lady Woodley had never asked her father to come here, even though she had spoken of him before.

"You and Lady Woodley were friends of a sort as children, weren't you?" she asked.

Her father's face filled with color and he shifted in his seat. "I-well-yes, I suppose. My father worked for her father and we were of an age, so we saw each other often."

"Then why be nervous, you are only meeting an old friend."

"Yes," his voice became far away. "An old friend."

She might have said more, addressed the strange expression on his handsome face, but at that moment the carriage door opened and she was greeted by the familiar face of one of Lady Woodley's footmen. He extended a hand to help her out of the rig.

As she took it, she said, "Good morning Thomas, thank you."

The young man flashed a brilliant smile at her. "Miss Gray."

Her father followed in her exit and the footman straightened up immediately. "Sir."

"Yes, yes," her father said, still shifting uncomfortably.

"Go on up, Vernon is waiting for you," Thomas said with another of those wide smiles for Juliet.

She swallowed hard as she took her father's arm and led him up the wide stairway to the door where the house butler, Vernon, awaited them.

"Good morning, Miss Gray," Vernon said with a rare flash of a small smile. "And Mr. Gray, I presume."

"Indeed," her father said and Juliet still heard the anxiousness in his voice. He was truly shaken by this invitation. And she had no idea why it troubled him so much.

"Lady Woodley is waiting for you in the Yellow Room," Vernon explained as he motioned for them to follow him down the hallway.

Juliet had been here so many times, she hardly noticed the opulence round them, but her father seemed taken in by all they saw as they walked up the hallway. He even dragged her back a bit as his stare flitted from art piece to art piece.

"She did marry well," he muttered.

"What?" Juliet whispered.

"Nothing," her father said with a shake of his head.

Juliet cast him a side glance as Vernon pushed opened the parlor door and stepped inside. "Mr. Gray and Miss Juliet Gray, my lady," he announced.

"Of course," came Lady Woodley's warm and welcoming voice. A voice that made Juliet smile every time she heard it. "Please come in."

Vernon stepped aside and Juliet drew her father into the room. It was a bright, happy room where Juliet knew Lady Woodley conducted mostly family gatherings and business. To be invited into this room meant the lady saw a person as close as family.

Juliet scanned the room swiftly, but their hostess was the only person in attendance. Gabriel was not with her. A fact that made Juliet's stomach stop fluttering, but also left her with a faint disappointment she shoved aside immediately.

"My lady," Juliet began, expecting Lady Woodley to offer her one of her welcoming smiles, perhaps a squeeze of the hand. But to her surprise, the lady wasn't looking at her, but behind her where her father had come to a halt in the doorway.

Juliet stepped back and looked between the two. Lady Woodley was pale as parchment paper, her lips thin and her eyes wide. And Juliet's father was just as pale, supporting himself against the doorjamb as if he couldn't stand on his own.

"Susanna," he finally whispered. "You have not changed, not in all these years."

His words seemed to break the spell, for Lady Woodley turned her face with a blush and a faint smile. "Nor have you, Jed."

Juliet stared at them. What in the world was happening? She had heard Lady Woodley speak warmly of her father, and she had suspected that perhaps there had once been a childish romantic interest between them, but now she saw a bald emotional connection that was as raw as it was intense.

She was an intruder here, apparently. More than she had ever suspected.

She shifted her attention to her father, trying to see him through new eyes. What Lady Woodley said was not true, of course. Her father *had* changed, certainly, even in just years since her mother's death. He was still strong of body and exceptionally sharp of mind, but his hair had gone gray ten years before and his face had been lined with faint grief and too many long nights fiddling with experiments and reading until dawn.

Still, Juliet had always thought him handsome. And apparently so did the lovely, fine boned, utterly sophisticated Lady Woodley.

Lady Woodley suddenly shook her head. "Mr. Gray. Of course I mean, Mr. Gray."

Her father blinked and he straightened up. "Lady Woodley, my apologies for my lack of manners."

Lady Woodley ignored the apology and motioned them to the small circle of chairs that were gathered around a low table where tea had been set.

"Would you like refreshments?" Lady Woodley asked, the only remnants of any emotion between them a slight tremor to her voice.

Slowly, Juliet approached one of the chairs and settled herself in. Her father did the same.

"None for me," Juliet said, caution in her tone. She suddenly felt like a chaperone and wasn't sure how to play the part.

Her father smiled. "A bit of tea would be lovely."

Lady Woodley cast him a quick glance and then poured before she swiftly added two sugars and a dash of milk to the brew. Juliet drew back. That was exactly how her father took his tea, twice a day for the last twenty-five years of her life and probably the entire span of his own.

Her father took the cup from Lady Woodley's suddenly shaking hand and took a small sip. "Perfect," he said softly.

Lady Woodley blushed, actually *blushed* and Juliet's hand tightened on her chair arm.

"Thank you for having us here today," Juliet said, trying to cut the tension a bit, if only for own sake. "You are looking very well."

"Thanks to you," Lady Woodley said, shifting her attention to Juliet and gifting her with one of those warm and motherly smiles that Juliet had come to crave since the first moment she had entered Lady Woodley's chamber. "Jed...Mr. Gray, you do know what a revelation your daughter is? What a gift?"

Juliet blushed as her father puffed up with pride. "It is always what I've said, my lady."

"Oh, you two," Juliet said with a shake of her head. "I did nothing out of the ordinary, Lady Woodley. I simply treated you and prayed that what I did would help. You fought the battle and should take the credit for your recovery."

The marchioness arched a fine brow. "You take too little

credit, not that I would expect otherwise. You are such a modest young woman and never ask for attention. But you are owed it, my dear, so I hope you will accept, once again, my most sincere gratitude."

Juliet tilted her head. There was no use having an argument with the lady. "I do, of course."

"I would like to repay you," Lady Woodley continued.

Juliet smoothed her hands on her dress reflexively. "I assure you that your son has paid all my fees in full and then some. You owe me nothing else."

"But I do," Lady Woodley said softly. "Juliet, I have come to see you not just as the healer who was called in to assist me, but as a friend. Even a daughter."

Juliet swallowed hard, blinking at the tears that leapt to her eyes even as she heard her father suck in a sharp breath through his teeth. "That means so much to me, my lady. More than you shall ever know."

Lady Woodley reached out and covered Juliet's hand with her own. "I have asked you and your father here today to make a proposition to you."

Juliet worried the inside of her cheek for a moment. "What sort of proposition?"

Lady Woodley's gaze slid to her father. "I would like to invite your daughter to accompany me to London for the upcoming holiday season. And because I know that you would not like to be separated from her for very long, you would be welcome to join us, as well."

Juliet shook her head. "I-I don't understand."

Lady Woodley smiled. "I would like you and your father to come and stay in my London home until the end of January. You will celebrate the Christmas holiday with our family and be my personal guest at some gatherings in the city. I would provide you with some new gowns, as well."

Juliet pushed from the settee and took a few steps away. Shock hit her in waves. She liked Lady Woodley so very much, but she had never thought that she was seen as a charity case by the woman.

"You do not look happy with this invitation," Lady Woodley said, rising to move toward her. "What is wrong?"

Juliet measured her tone carefully. "My lady, I could not possibly take your charity-"

Lady Woodley's eyes went wide. "You misunderstand me, Juliet. I don't see this as charity in the slightest. I *like* you, my dear and I want to give you a reward for your kindness and your assistance to me."

Juliet shook her head. The idea of going to London, of parading around in the titled elite and being displayed made her very skin crawl. Aside from which, if she was staying with Lady Woodley in her home over the holidays, she would certainly be put in the path of Gabriel more than once.

A traitorous part of her soared at that thought and then she pushed the reaction away. She didn't want that. And she knew he likely wanted it even less.

"I couldn't intrude, then," she began.

Lady Woodley let out a soft sound of frustration and turned her attention back to Juliet's father. "Jed-Mr. Gray, you must help me to persuade your dearest daughter that this is a good course of action for you both!"

Juliet narrowed her gaze at her father, hoping to send him the strong message that he should take her side. But she found a thoughtful look on his face as he examined first her and then Lady Woodley.

"Juliet, you should consider this offer," he finally said slowly. "You work so hard on the behalf of all those in the village, and you take such good care of me. I like the idea of you having time to yourself, a pleasure just for you."

Juliet watched him closely. He was still casting side glances at Lady Woodley and she realized that while he was speaking the truth about wanting her to be happy, he was also incapable of hiding how much this renewed acquaintance with his old 'friend' meant to him.

Could she deny him his chance to spend more time with Lady Woodley if it meant so much to him?

She sighed. "I-I just don't know."

Lady Woodley's smile was triumphant, as if she knew she had already won. "Then allow me to know for both of us! I have already arranged for the seamstress in the village to measure you this afternoon in order to make several gowns for you."

"Evelyn Wilcox?" Juliet asked, blinking in surprise.

"That is the one. She made my new daughter-in-law Josie's wedding dress for her ceremony with Evan just a few months ago and did wonderful work. She will have the gowns sent to London by the time you arrive."

Juliet gasped. "I feel as though you are sweeping me away."

Lady Woodley laughed and then reached out to grasp both of Juliet's hands. "Then allow me to sweep you, my dear! I want to do this, please let me!"

Juliet explored the lady's face, saw the earnestness there. Then she glanced at her father and saw the flicker of hope in his stare, not just for her, but for himself.

She sighed. "I-oh, very well. You are impossible to refuse."

Lady Woodley nodded once before she drew Juliet in for an unexpected but warm hug. "My children tell me that constantly! Oh, I am so pleased that you will do this. Now you must hurry. Miss Wilcox expects you almost directly. And I will send all the details along to you before Gabriel and I leave for London tomorrow."

Juliet stiffened at the mention of his name. A reminder of what she would be walking into when she joined Lady Woodley. But then, he would be staying at his own home. And perhaps he would simply be too busy to call overly much.

She would just have to hope that would be true. Otherwise, it could be a very long visit, indeed.

Other Books by Jess Michaels

THE WICKED WOODLEYS

Forbidden (Book 1)

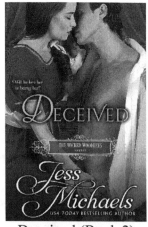

Deceived (Book 2)

THE NOTORIOUS FLYNNS
The Other Duke (Book 1)
The Scoundrel's Lover (Book 2)
The Widow Wager (Book 3)
No Gentleman for Georgina (Book 4)
A Marquis for Mary (Book 5)

THE LADIES BOOK OF PLEASURES
A Matter of Sin
A Moment of Passion
A Measure of Deceit

THE PLEASURE WARS SERIES
Taken By the Duke
Pleasuring The Lady
Beauty and the Earl
Beautiful Distraction

MISTRESS MATCHMAKER SERIES
An Introduction to Pleasure
For Desire Alone
Her Perfect Match

ALBRIGHT SISTERS SERIES
Everything Forbidden
Something Reckless
Taboo
Nothing Denied

Jess Michaels raffles a FREE Kindle or Amazon gift certificate EVERY month to members of her newsletter, so sign up on her website:
http://www.authorjessmichaels.com/join-the-jess-michaels-newsletter/

About the Author

Jess Michaels writes erotic historical romance from her home in Tucson, AZ. She has three assistants: One cat that blocks the screen, one that is very judgmental and her husband that does all the heavy lifting. She has written over 50 books, enjoys long walks in the desert and once wrestled a bear over a piece of pie. One of these things is a lie.

Jess loves to hear from fans! So please feel free to contact her in any of the following ways (or carrier pigeon):
www.AuthorJessMichaels.com
PO Box 814, Cortaro, AZ 85652-0814

Email: Jess@AuthorJessMichaels.com
Twitter www.twitter.com/JessMichaelsbks
Facebook: www.facebook.com/JessMichaelsBks

Jess Michaels raffles a FREE Kindle or Amazon gift certificate EVERY month to members of her newsletter, so sign up on her website:
http://www.authorjessmichaels.com/join-the-jess-michaels-newsletter/

Made in the USA
Middletown, DE
26 April 2016